Baynard's List

Jason Vail

Baynard's List

ISBN-13: 978-1463623166
ISBN-10: 146362316X

Hawk Publishing
Tallahassee, FL 32312

Baynard's List

Ludlow

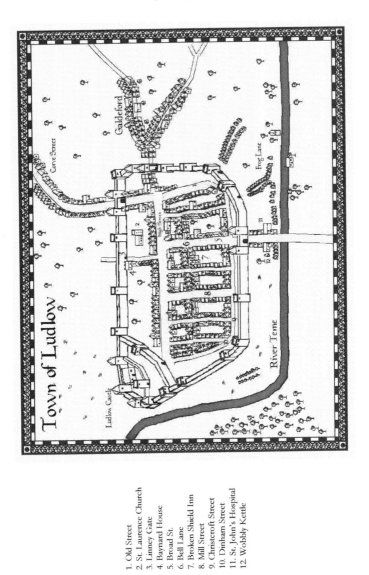

1. Old Street
2. St. Laurence Church
3. Linney Gate
4. Baynard House
5. Broad St.
6. Bell Lane
7. Broken Shield Inn
8. Mill Street
9. Christcroft Street
10. Dinham Street
11. St. John's Hospital
12. Wobbly Kettle

Ludlow
England

October 1262

Baynard's List

Chapter 1

"If you expect me to save you from the gallows, you must tell me everything. Do you understand? Everything!"

Ademar de Valence, justice to his Grace Henry, the third of his name, king of England and recently returned to power, regarded the felon slumped before him. They were in one of the jail cells at Ludlow castle, a large commodious fortress on the border with that wild country inhabited by the unruly Welsh.

The room itself was a filthy sty tucked against the east wall of the outer bailey beside the stables. It stank of feces, piss and wet soil. Flies swarmed about in the late October air. The prisoner sat cross-legged on the bare ground, connected to an iron ring in the wall by a metal leash and collar. He was a big man with huge shoulders and a thick neck. He wore expensive looking hose and a stylish black coat. The clothes were soiled and torn, but no one had yet relieved the coat of its silver buttons and he had a large silver signet ring for sealing letters on his right index finger, which gave evidence that he had some education, odd in so obvious a ruffian. Outside, strutting around on the street, he had presented an imposing figure, but here, chained to the wall, he looked rather more like a whipped St. Bernard. Valence felt a momentary stab of pity for him. Perhaps it was the fellow's resemblance to a dog. Valence was fond of dogs.

The man, whose name was Clement, nodded mutely. From the look on his face, Valence expected Clement to throw himself prostrate and plead for his life. Valence wouldn't have minded that bit of desperation; normally he had no use for pleading, but he wanted Clement firmly in his grip.

Valence said, "So — you killed him, that poor carter."A carter named Patrick had been stabbed to death a month ago at a tavern across the River Teme. Clement stood accused of the murder based on some thin evidence and clever deduction.

For a moment, it appeared that Clement would not confess, that perhaps he had some spine after all. But then he muttered, "Yessir."

"Impressive, most impressive," Valence murmured reluctantly, fingering his chin.

Clement gaped. "Sir? It is?"

Valence was insulted the wretch had spoken. "No, you idiot, not that you killed him. That you were caught. By God's blood you should have got away with it." Valence had no sympathy for murderers, but he reserved special contempt for failures.

"Yessir."

"Hardly a shred of evidence connecting you . . ." Valence said thoughtfully.

"No shred, sir, no shred at all. Weren't no evidence. We were careful."

Valence nodded in understanding if not approval. According to the gossips, Clement's master, Ancelin Baynard, had a bastard daughter. The carter had attempted to arrange a marriage between his son and the daughter. Baynard had objected. A quarrel had erupted between them, and at Baynard's behest, Clement killed the carter. It was a sordid and small affair, one he would not ordinarily give more than five minutes attention. Something else had brought Valence here, something Clement had mentioned in his secret letter to the justice. For Baynard had been rather more than a prosperous draper. He had, in fact, been an intelligencer for the crown, whose task was to gather information about supporters of the faction of barons opposing the king. Valence said briskly, "Now, as to the list, tell me about that."

Clement's tongue flicked over his lips. "Well, it's two lists, really. Master Baynard kept one showing all the king's men in the area, those who had pledged loyalty, especially those who'd done so in secret."

"In secret?" Valence murmured, unable to conceal his eagerness to hear more. There was a war brewing in England. Most people weren't aware of it, but it had already broken out beneath the skin of ordinary existence. It was a shadowy war at present, fought by the spies and agents of the antagonists. On the one hand was the king and his party, which were united behind that feckless, weak, and indecisive man by the promise of the gain that always showered from the fingers of the grateful monarch. On the other were mostly petty barons, merchants and townsfolk who dominated this blithering new assembly called Parliament, who saw corruption and misrule when they gazed toward Westminster, and who had the temerity to wish for something better. They would have been nothing, these opponents of the royal will, except for Simon de Montfort. An earl and the king's brother-in-law, Montfort was an odd partisan for reform, but the king's jealousy and mishandling of a trivial dispute over the dowery of Montfort's wife had driven him into the arms of men who would put shackles of restraint on God's anointed sovereign. What folly to risk a throne over a sister's dowery. But Henry's judgment had always led him to be generous with those he should not and parsimonious with those he should cultivate.

Valence knew about this shadow war, of course, but he was not privy to it. He was not sure why. He regarded himself as a man of ability who had much to contribute to the king's cause. That he had been overlooked or ignored rankled his pride.

But opportunity had fallen into his lap. The identity of the master spy in the west of England had been revealed to him — who would have thought it was a mere draper like Anselin Baynard. Moreover, Baynard himself was dead, murdered in revenge by the carter's son. That left an important scrap of parchment on the loose. If it fell into the wrong hands great damage could be done to the king's interests.

"Yes, sir," Clement said. "Some of them were well placed to inform on Montfort's people. He said they were not to be exposed to danger."

"But he listed them."

"To keep track of how much we — he — paid them for their services."

"He had to pay men to secure their loyalty?"

"Well, they were in the king's employ, or that's how he characterized it. And they had expenses, you see."

"Hmm. I should like to see those accounts. Money wasted probably. There always is. And what of the other list?"

"It contained the names of the men he had determined joined the barons' party."

"I take it these loyalties were not publicly known either."

"Some were, most weren't."

"Where would the list be?"

"Master Baynard kept it in his writing box."

"Just like that? A valuable list whose exposure could lead to the deaths of men? Slapped into a writing box?"

"Well, he kept it locked." Clement's face darkened and for an instant a frightened expression passed over it.

"What?" Valence said.

"Sir?"

"What was that look for?"

"Someone got into the box."

Valence was alarmed. "Who?"

"That deputy coroner," Clement said with some venom. "Attebrook." It was understandable that Clement might bear some hard feelings for Stephen Attebrook. It was Attebrook whose investigation had identified Clement as the carter's murderer. Had it not been for Stephen Attebrook, Clement would not have been rotting in this stink of a jail awaiting trial for murder.

"How do you know this?" Valence asked.

"He got inside the writing box during his inquiry into . . . the carter's death. There was a note sent to Master Baynard by the carter's boy to lure him out of the house to his death. Attebrook was looking for that."

"Attebrook didn't take the list?" Valence said, trying to conceal his anxiety.

"No. It was still there when I looked."

Valence relaxed somewhat. "How did he get into the box if it was locked?"

"I don't know. I expect he picked the lock. He's a clever one. And if it wasn't him, it was his clerk, Gilbert."

Valence was not relieved to hear that this precious box was not safe from casual thieves. "Where is the box?"

"It should be in the master's study. Was the last time I was there."

"I see." Valence folded his thin, claw-like hands in thought. "That was weeks ago. Just before you were arrested."

"It was."

Valence rose abruptly from his stool. He felt suddenly as if there was not a moment to lose, although he had already wasted almost a month before appreciating the acuteness of this crisis. "Thank you, Clement. You have been most helpful."

Clement reached out for the hem of Valence's scarlet, fox-trimmed robe. "You'll help me then, sir?"

Valence thought momentarily, and with some relish, of the consternation he could inflict by rejecting the plea. But instead, he took Clement's hand and drew him up as far as the leash would allow. Clement had been a useful servant to Baynard, and might now be useful to him. Valence said, "I will protect you, Master Clement. But you must swear loyalty to me, and to me alone."

Clement nearly wept. "Thank you, sir. I will."

"My, you are a mess, Master Clement," Valence said distastefully, wrinkling his nose as the two of them emerged into yellow autumn sunlight. "We shall have to get you cleaned up and presentable."

Clement massaged his neck where the iron ring, which he had worn for nearly a month, had left a deep raw mark. "Thank you, sir."

Walter Henle, the deputy sheriff in this part of Herefordshire, came hurrying toward them across the enormous outer bailey of Ludlow castle. Apparently you couldn't keep anything secret, although how he could have found out so quickly about Clement's release Valence could not fathom. Henle looked anxious. Valence and Clement were already striding toward the main gate. Henle fell in beside them. "M-m-my lord," he stammered. "What's going on? Why is that man loose?"

"He is released on my authority," Valence said, whose authority as a king's circuit justice was considerable, certainly sufficient to secure the release of accused murderers. "He has been helpful to the crown, and I require his further services."

"But, sir, he's a murderer."

"An accused murderer, Henle. And regardless if he is guilty or not, he may win a pardon for his services to the crown. That will be all," Valence snapped.

Henle stopped pursuing Valence, his hands flapping in dismay and his mouth working like a fish, but emitting no sound.

Valence had already forgotten about Henle. He had other, very urgent matters on his mind. With Clement at his heels, he passed through the narrow main gate into High Street, a broad thoroughfare that ran almost two hundred yards along the top of the ridge that formed the spine of the town, narrowing only when it reached Broad Street and the parish church, St. Laurence's. He marched as fast as he could go, and as he was a tall and very thin, man, his strides were long, and he was capable of surprising speed. Clement nearly had to jog on his shorter legs to keep up with him.

High Street was nearly deserted, this being the middle of a non-market day, but the sight of Valence hurrying at top speed was so unusual that those who were about did not fail to pause to watch this strange procession. When he came abreast of the goldsmith Leofwine Wattepas' house at the corner with Mill Street, his mob of apprentices stopped work to gape through the open windows. Valence could hear Wattepas' annoyed voice ordering them back to work. Valence nodded a good day to Wattepas, who was dimly visible inside, without breaking stride.

Where Broad Street met High, there was a narrow lane to the left that ran straight north to a small gate in the town wall. Valence swooped round the corner into that lane, his robes billowing about his skinny legs, looking like a crow making a sharp turn. A crowd of boys emerging from the church school to take their dinners scattered like quail at his approach and the thunderous look on his face, although schoolboys were not known for their tendency to respect their elders when assembled in one of their packs. But the urgency on Valence's face, the obvious wealth reflected in his clothes, and the thickset ruffian at his heels must have persuaded the boys that this was one man they did not want to ruffle.

Baynard's house was the last on the left before the wall. It was a big house as befitted a wealthy merchant, for Baynard in life had been one of the town's leading drapers, a man so rich that he held not one but three houses in the town. This was the house he had lived in, a three-story mansion, the ground floor walls made of stone, capped with three timber and plaster upper stories.

Valence did not knock on the door. He stood aside, an indication for Clement, who lived here, to hold it for him. Clement was a moment taking the hint, but he got it soon enough.

Valence entered as briskly as he had charged down High Street, passing two large rooms at the front which in an ordinary merchant's house would have contained the shop, but here were fitted out as a cloak room and sitting room. Beyond was the great hall, which stretched nearly the length of the house, concluding at a massive fireplace so large that two men could have lain in it head to foot. To the right was another, not quite so massive, fireplace which would have served well by itself in any other house. The floor was made of wood, not the customary dirt, and the interior timbers were painted blue, red and yellow. Green glass in the windows imparted a rather sickly hue to the whole. Valence was annoyed at the richness of the setting. It mocked his own circumstances. He was a cousin to William de Valence, earl of

Pembroke, and had taken William's name. As a Valence, he had been awarded estates when he came to England, but they were not as fine as he expected. He hated merchants like Baynard who had more than he.

A wiry man with a thick mop of graying black hair hurried across the hall to meet them. His astonishment at the intrusion was plain. His eyes darted from Valence to Clement and back again. He managed to get out, "My lord —"

But Valence interrupted him. "Where is the library?"

The wiry man blinked and pointed above and behind Valence. Valence turned and saw he was indicating a corner room on the second floor overlooking the street. "Thank you," Valence said, and swept toward the stairway, which descended by the huge stone fireplace.

"Clement," the wiry man said as he fell in behind the pair, "what's going on?"

"I'll explain later, William," Clement said nastily. "Get out of the way and shut up."

"Oh, dear."

The path to the library led along a catwalk overlooking the hall, for the interior space rose to the roof. Valence's footsteps echoed in the hall like little claps of thunder. Servants had come out of the rear of the house at the commotion and were staring at him, and the rustle of whispers reached Valence's ears as he halted momentarily at the library door. He put his hand on the latch, lifted it, and went in.

The library was a small corner room, about eight feet by ten, and well lighted by windows overlooking the street and the side yard. It was sparsely furnished. There was a shelf full of a dozen or so books and a table. On the table was the writing box, a slanted piece of polished wood on which one did the writing, supported by panels to form the box. Valence put his hands on the lid and lifted. It was locked. That was good.

"Where's the key?" he asked.

William gulped and shook his head.

Clement said, "The master had the only key. It should be with his things."

"Well, fetch it, then," Valence said impatiently.

Clement hurried out.

The other fellow, that man William, lingered in the doorway. He had an anxious way of looking at his feet and then out the window, and back again. Valence was used to anxiety in servants, so he took no special notice.

"Who are you?" Valence asked.

"Muryet," he said. "William Muryet. I'm the butler, and I also act as my lady's chamberlain."

Valence suppressed a snort at Muryet's reference to the woman of the house as a lady. That term only belonged to women of the gentry. Olivia Baynard had been gentry once, but she had lost her inheritance when her brother was executed for embezzling crown funds. Destitute and desperate, she had married this merchant. As far as Valence was concerned, such a marriage took her out of the gentry and forfeited her right to call herself a lady. He snapped, "Then do what good butlers and chamberlains do. Be hospitable."

"Yessir. I'll bring some wine, sir. Right away, sir." Muryet backed out and disappeared.

Good. That got rid of the man. Valence could hear the hurried thuds of his feet as he hastened away.

Valence sat down at the table. From this vantage point, he could see up College Lane to St. Laurence's church. The street was deserted, except for a cat doing its business by the churchyard gate. A dog emerged from an alley a short distance away and saw the cat. It let out a happy yip and went to investigate the cat. This cat was no friend of dogs. It arched its back and hissed. The dog broke into a lope, and the cat ran away. Valence hoped the dog caught the cat and tore it to pieces. He hated cats.

Clement reappeared and held out a small bronze key. "There you go, sir."

"Out of the way," Valence said. He put the key in the lock. It fit perfectly. The lock yielded with a snap. Feeling the breath coming quicker in his throat, Valence slowly lifted the lid to the box. Once he had the list in his possession, he would report this feat to Westminster, which would be grateful and certainly would reward him handsomely for his enterprise in protecting the king's interests. Valence would propose himself as Baynard's replacement, not to manage the dirty, day-to-day business of spying himself, but as a suitable watchman over the master spy and keeper of the king's business in these parts who would take all the credit — and garner the rewards — for the spy's work.

The box was filled with velum sheets and parchments, over which trickled writing in an unexpectedly neat hand. It was the casual writing learned in church school and not the clerk hand Valence was used to, but elegant nonetheless. He lifted the documents out of the box one by one, examining each one closely. Some of them were barely more than scribbles and appeared to be reports from Baynard's informants. Others looked like notes taken of oral reports or drafts of messages Baynard planned to send to whoever was his superior. Valence reached the bottom of the box without finding anything that looked like a list of names.

"I don't see it," Valence said, unable to keep the alarm and disappointment from his voice. "You look. Show me which one it is."

Clement spread the documents on the table.

"Well?" Valence demanded.

"It's not here," Clement said.

"You assured me it was!" Valence shouted. Clement's letter had been emphatic about this detail, and he was incensed to find the promise was untrue. "What happened to it?"

Clement flinched as if he had been struck. "I don't know, sir. I swear. I saw it. It was here after Attebrook got in the box. Now?" He shrugged helplessly.

Valence had a vision of the royal reaction at this news. It might be possible to conceal the disaster, but Valence didn't believe that. King Henry would find out somehow. As soon as he heard of Baynard's death, he'd be sure to dispatch an agent to put together the scattered threads of Baynard's network. The agent would learn of Valence's involvement. There'd be no concealing it. The servants had seen him and they'd talk. Instead of the rewards Valence anticipated, Henry would be angry. He might even blame Valence for the loss. The thought frightened him.

"I must find it," Valence said grimly. "I must."

Chapter 2

"Waste of good salt if you ask me," said Harry the legless beggar.

"Nobody's asking you," said Stephen Attebrook, impoverished knight and part time deputy coroner. He watched as Jennie Wistwode poured salt into the steaming bucket of water at his feet and then stirred it with a big wooden spoon. The dissolving salt gave the water a gray, slate-like sheen, then the water cleared as the whirlpool in its center dissipated.

Jennie straightened up and said, "Careful, that's hot."

"Hope you cook yourself, you idiot," Harry grumbled. He looked up at Jennie and held out his bowl of Edith Wistwode's famous mutton pie, which Jennie had brought out to the pair of them shortly before she had fetched the bucket of water. "You wouldn't have any left to spare, would you?"

"You've got all you're entitled to," Jennie snapped. "The dish is spiced enough." Then her round, plain face lightened up with a great smile for Stephen. "Go ahead, your honor, you don't want to wait too long. It only works when the water's hot."

Stephen pulled the boot from his bad foot, reluctant to let the others see the stump, for half the foot was missing, chopped off by a Moor during an assault on a castle in Spain, where he had spent nearly the last ten years fighting a war on the borders that never seemed to end. He had made a fortune in Spain, but in the end he had lost the fortune, his woman, and all his friends. Now he had nothing but his armor, three horses, and some tatty clothes.

He eased the foot into the bucket, wincing at the heat, which was fairly scalding. He had been training with soldiers from the castle garrison, and his bad foot felt as though he had been pounding it on rocks. He also had a blossoming bruise on his cheek where one of the castle squires had landed a good blow with a wooden practice sword — just when the bruises from his duel a few weeks ago had begun to disappear.

"How's that?" Jennie asked.

"Good," Stephen said, forcing a smile over gritted teeth, which caused her smile to grow even larger. "Thanks."

"You're welcome," she said. It appeared that she would have stood there longer, but her mother, Edith, called from a side window of the Broken Shield Inn, and reluctantly, with a backward glance, Jennie took her leave and returned to work.

Harry looked disgusted even while he filled his face with mutton pie. "She's sweet on you," he said with a full mouth. "She come to your room yet?"

Stephen lived in a small room at the top and rear of the inn, the open window of which was visible from their position, Stephen on a bench and Harry on the ground, at the door to the stables.

"None of your damn business," Stephen said tartly. Harry was right; he was liable to cook himself in this water. It hurt so that he could barely keep his foot in the bucket. He had to admit, though, it did seem to make a difference. The heat eased the knotted muscles. He could almost feel it seeping around the toes which weren't there. Often he could still feel those missing toes. Sometimes they itched, sometimes they hurt, often sharply. But now the missing toes, and the rest of his foot, seemed to relax, as if the foot was dissolving in the hot water along with the salt.

Harry grunted in reply and absently picked a leaf and then a twig from the matted mass of beard of his, a gross tangle of brown hair that hung like a bib to his chest. The thing, in fact, was even useful as a bib, as Harry proved when he wiped his lips on the end of the beard.

Stephen noticed that Harry's eyes had followed Jennie as she disappeared through the side door to the inn. For a moment, Stephen thought he saw Harry's eyes alight with wistfulness. Stephen had the sudden inspiration that Harry was sweet on Jennie. Could he be jealous of her attentions to him? It was an astonishing notion. It had never occurred to him that Harry might be interested in Jennie. Unlike some men, Harry never talked about women as regards to himself, although Stephen was aware that he had once had a wife who had vanished after his accident, which had taken his legs above the knees a few years back. His lord had thrown him out because he couldn't work, and now he was a beggar.

Stephen was painfully aware of how women were disgusted with deformity, and his own was comparatively small and generally concealable. It was bad enough for Harry that he had no legs, but to be a beggar besides made him the least desirable of men, not to mention the fact that he lived in the stables, even though behind that matted beard Stephen suspected there lurked a very presentable face. Stephen felt sorry for Harry, but didn't dare show it. Harry had nothing but scorn for pity, and Harry in a scornful mood was a dragon.

So Stephen said, "But no, if you must know. She hasn't."

"Probably thinks she can do better," Harry sniffed as his spoon went into his mouth.

Probably she can, Stephen thought but did not say so. He had lost the best woman he had ever had — had ever hoped to have — to a fever in Spain, and he felt as though he would never be able to fill the yawning chasm that her death had left. The truth was, Stephen himself was not much of a prize. Although he had been born into the gentry, a family that held lands not far from Ludlow, he had fallen pretty low. He had nothing now but his arms — such good as they did since he wasn't much up to soldiering these days — three horses, and a position as deputy coroner of this part of the county and the town that barely paid enough to keep the horses in fodder, and winter was on its way and he needed new shoes and a coat. He had nothing now that would interest a decent woman. He wasn't so bad looking, except for the foot, or so he had been told, nearly six feet tall and lean and muscular with jet black hair, but decent women didn't pick their men on how they looked but on what they had.

"Look at you, holes in your stockings," Harry went on after gulping his spoonful of pie. "Boots all worn out. Shameful, I'd say."

"That's enough, Harry."

"What's wrong, can't stand the truth?"

"You know, Harry," Stephen said mildly, "I've often wondered why someone hasn't bothered to cut off your head to match your legs." Talking to Harry was like fencing, only with tongues. If you didn't defend yourself, he'd cut you to ribbons.

"Oh, they've tried, but I'm too fast for them." Harry put his empty bowl on the bench and indicated Stephen's, which sat barely touched beside him. "You done with that?"

"I reckon so," Stephen sighed. "Go ahead."

Harry eagerly snatched up Stephen's bowl while Stephen removed his foot from the bucket, as the water had already begun to cool. The shock of the autumn air on his wet foot almost made him gasp. He toweled off his leg with his stocking, which he drew on. He turned for his boot to find Harry poking a finger through a hole in the sole. "Here, Harry," Stephen beckoned.

Harry tossed the boot at him then climbed onto his board, a flat piece of wood with rockers on the bottom that Gilbert had made for him some time ago. With padded gloves on his knuckles, the board helped him move about more easily. Harry flexed his fingers inside the gloves. "That hits the spot, wouldn't you say? No, you can't, since you didn't eat enough to feed a bird. Too bad for you. Well, back to work. See you this evening."

And Harry began to swing himself across the back yard toward the gate with a speed that had not yet ceased to astonish Stephen.

"See you, Harry."

Stephen settled back down on the bench and took up his bread, which Harry had not asked for. He tore off a piece and put it in his mouth. It was good bread, baked this morning, and still soft enough almost to melt in his mouth. But it seemed tasteless. Jennie and the conversation with Harry had provoked memories of Spain and loss, and Stephen felt heavy with melancholy. Lately, he had been able to go a full day, or even two at a time, without thinking of Spain and Taresa and all that was gone and would never be regained.

A commotion at the inn broke into his thoughts — someone talking loud and excitedly, although he could not make out what was being said. Stephen was about to rise to see what was the matter when the side door to the Broken Shield burst open, and Gilbert Wistwode emerged and rushed across the yard in his distinctive waddling trot. His round face under its fringe of gray hair was grim.

Gilbert skidded to a halt before Stephen. Stephen opened his mouth to ask what was wrong, but Gilbert spoke first. He said, "There's been an accident."

Stephen had begun to shrink at hearing those words because it meant that someone had died. Death was a common thing in this world, and Stephen, like most people, was fairly hardened to it. But death still managed to fascinate, to frighten, and to sadden, and if you didn't stare at it as though a carnival had come to town, you just passed it by with a wag of the head and a prayer and tried to forget about it because it wasn't someone you loved. But Stephen could not just pass it by. His very job was about death. It had, he once thought in a quiet moment under the blankets in his room upstairs, been about death since he was seventeen and become a soldier, nine long years ago, although at the time he had not seen it that way — it had seemed then about excitement and glory and the prospect of plunder. Now it was about death in another way. He had to look death in the face as he had never had to before and to pronounce the manner and the reason for it, so that there would be an official record and the death could be properly assessed, because no man, woman, or child was supposed to pass into the next world without giving fine to the king for the misfortune.

"Where?" Stephen asked.

"On Corve Street by St. Leonard's," Gilbert said.

The little chapel of St. Leonard's lay not quite a quarter mile north of Corve Gate. He could ride, but in the time it would take to curry, brush, and saddle the mare, they could be at St. Leonard's doors. "Close enough to walk, I suppose."

"Does your foot feel up to it?"

"I'm all right. Jennie's tonic was a charm."

Gilbert smiled, pleased. Jennie was his daughter. "She's a good girl."

"It's a good thing she takes after her mother and not you."

Gilbert grinned ruefully and rubbed his short round nose that looked like a cork sticking out of an ale barrel. It had been Jennie's good fortune not to be blessed with that nose. He said, "So it is. The boys wouldn't pay a wit of attention to her if she did." He shook his head. "A constant worry that is, though. You have no idea how much trouble a daughter is."

"How can I not know? You keep reminding me."

As they turned toward the gate, Gilbert said, "One of these days, God willing, you'll find out. Then you'll rue the day you ever said a cross word to me."

Fat chance of that, Stephen thought sourly. "I? Speak crossly to you? When have I ever done so?"

They passed through the gate into Bell Lane, a narrow street wide enough to allow passage of one cart at a time. The ground was muddy from last night's rain.

Gilbert said, "How did you get that bruise? Run into a door again?"

"Something like that."

"You ought to be more careful. You'll break your head one day."

"My mother used to tell me that."

"Wise woman, your mother. I never knew her, of course, but she clearly was passingly wise. Especially having turned you out before you burned down the house."

Stephen laughed. "I almost did that once."

Gilbert's eyebrows arched and his mouth formed a questioning Oh.

Stephen had no choice now but to go on. If he didn't, Gilbert would wheedle the story out of him. "My brother dared me to climb onto the roof. It was thatched then and gave way under me. I fell by the hearth and a large bundle of thatch came with me and landed in the fire. It burned a hole in the floor before the servants put it out."

"Oh, my," Gilbert chuckled.

Stephen frowned slightly at the memory. It sounded rather funny now, but at the time there had been nothing funny about it. Father had been furious with him, but then, father had been angry at just about everything Stephen had done, as if there was nothing he could do right. "I think my father was more angry at the hole in the roof than the one in the floor. He'd been resisting mother's demands for a new slate roof, you see, and since something had to be done about the hole, he found his position weakened. So we got a slate roof out of the mishap."

"And you got a beating."

"Yes."

"Served you right."

"It paid for the roof."

Despite the easy talk, they had been walking fast, and by this time had reached the wide crossroad where Old Street and Draper's Row came together. The cattle market was held here, but today the crossroads was deserted except for a couple of carts creaking through, one piled with hay and the other holding several barrels and a few odd sticks of lumber.

They nodded greetings to the warden on his stool guarding Corve Gate and passed through into the suburb beyond. Years past, the land here had been largely in field, where townspeople had grazed sheep and cattle or grown hay, but now the street was lined with houses, their fronts smack on the verge and planted close together so that they almost seemed to form a solid wall of prosperous looking buildings.

As they rounded the curve of the street toward St. Leonard's, a crowd of twenty or so people came into view clustered in front of a timber-framed house on the right. It was a fairly quiet crowd, which was not unexpected, most people either gawking at a spectacle that only they could see or talking to each other in low voices, although, oddly, a few people were actually smiling and one or two laughing.

"Make way, make way," Gilbert said loudly as they reached the rear of the crowd. "Make way for the deputy coroner."

The crowd edged apart as Gilbert and Stephen came forward. They paused at the head of an alley so narrow that a man could spread out his arms and practically touch both neighboring buildings at once. A substantial rain barrel blocked the entrance. As Stephen squeezed around it, he glanced into the black water and thought for a moment he saw a fish in its depths. But that was silly. No one put fish in rain barrels.

Once he got by the barrel, he came upon what people had been gawking at. It was a crumpled thing that had once been a small man. He lay at the foot of some stairs running up the side of one of the houses in such an impossibly awkward position that there was no doubt he was dead. He could have been sitting against the wall, except his chest was toward the wall rather than away from it. His legs were crossed above the knees, and the knees themselves bent at sharp angles. One arm was under him and the other crooked behind his back but because of his position appeared as if it was in his lap. It was the man's head that was the worst. Instead of facing the wall, as it should have done, it had been turned clear around and hung down as if the back had become the chest and he was merely resting.

Stephen knelt by the body but did not touch it. Graying hair streaked with black hung down like ratty curtains, concealing the face. Stephen's mouth went suddenly dry. Although he could not yet see the dead man's face except for his rather pointed chin, Stephen guessed at his identity. Stephen gingerly parted one wing of his hair and pushed it out of the way behind an ear. The dead man's face, never known to have much color in life, had even less now — a grayish waxy pallor that reminded Stephen of a Roman statue he had seen once in Spain. The eyes were open, their natural deep brown dimmed by the odd film that always seemed to form over the eyes of the dead a short while after they had died. The eye lids were slightly down and, in cooperation with a open but slack mouth, gave the dead man a rather stupid expression that he had never worn when alive. There were cuts upon the face: through an eyebrow, across the nose, a split lip, upon the cheeks and chin. The split lip was particularly nasty, as if someone had parted it with scissors or a knife, and there was blood between the teeth. But altogether, the dead man had not bled much.

Stephen touched the man's face at the hinge of the jaw. The flesh was cold and the muscles there were rigid. He felt the man's hand. It was rigid also. The dead man's heavy wool coat was still wet from last evening's rain. The drizzle had stopped sometime before midnight, which meant that he had died before then.

He looked up at Gilbert, who was standing by with folded hands. He said, "Do you recognize him too?"

Gilbert nodded. "William Muryet, Ancelin Baynard's butler. A most unpleasant little man, although I hesitate to speak ill of the dead."

"Go ahead. He can't hear you. Hell's a long way off."

Gilbert sighed. "Well, Master Muryet owed us money. He has — or had — run up a rather sizeable bill at the Shield and paid only with excuses. It had got so bad that Edith was contemplating legal action." He shuddered at the prospect of lawyers. "He owed many people a great deal of money, if the rumors are to be believed."

"Then the rest of town will be as sorry at his death as you seem to be. Now they won't be paid back."

"They might if he left an estate," Gilbert said dryly.

"Well, don't rush off to secure it, pitiful as it probably is — a few stray coins in a purse under his pillow, if anything. We've work to do here."

"Speaking of work, I wonder what he was doing here."

"Not paying off his debts, I'm sure."

"Probably not."

Stephen straightened up and addressed the crowd. "Who owns this house?" He gestured to the house that sported the stairs leading to a door on the third story.

A tall, red-haired man named William Brandone had been watching in the crowd. He was a juryman in the town and the parish of Ludford. It was the duty of the jurymen to investigate the circumstances of any death in their district, report the facts to the coroner at the inquest, and collectively then to judge the manner and method of the death. He spoke up, "Mistress Helen Webbere, sir."

"Good day, William," Stephen said. Brandone was a candlemaker in the town, and although not well to do, he was a respected craftsman. "Would you mind asking her if she would kindly donate the use of her table for viewing the body."

Brandone nodded to the man beside him, another juryman, who pushed through the crowd toward Mistress Webbere's door.

"Who was the first finder?" Stephen asked Brandone, who had obviously been here for some time.

"Mistress Webbere's son, a boy of eight. Name of Ivo. Says he was sent to fetch water and spied the body in the alley. Says he didn't think much of it at first, that it was a beggar just sitting there. Went past it twice, and only on the third time noticed anything wrong."

"Told his mother, did he? And she summoned the watch?"

"Yes, sir," Brandone said.

"And you found out about it and came right out."

"That's right, sir."

"How long have you been here?"

"An hour now."

Stephen approved of Brandone's diligence. Jury service often meant a considerable sacrifice for small craftsmen like him. He obviously took his civic duty seriously. "Been asking questions? The usual inquiry?"

Brandone nodded.

Stephen was relieved. That meant he didn't have to make inquiries of his own. This unpleasant business might be concluded in short order. But then the import of that Brandone had told him finally registered. "No one saw or heard anything, did they?"

"Not that we've found so far, and we've talked to everyone in the houses all round."

Stephen looked up and down the stairway. "Not even Mistress Webbere or anyone in her family?"

"No, sir, so they say."

"What do you think happened, William?"

"I think he was drunk and fell down the stairs, sir."

Stephen eyed Brandone narrowly for a moment, then bent down and sniffed close to Muryet's face. Sure enough, the sour smell of bad wine lingered about him, although the smell was not strong. "He doesn't reek enough to suggest he'd been drinking so heavily he'd be liable for a fall."

Brandone said, "Or perhaps not drunk, but still fell down the stairs anyway. There's a loose step near the top."

"Is there," Stephen said.

He paid closer attention to the stairway now. It was just a series of wooden planks for steps set on a slender timber scaffold. It was obviously an old set of stairs, the wood gray and weathered and covered with moss in spots. Here and there some of the planks had been replaced with newer wood that wasn't so gray and in a couple of instances was yellow and new. Stephen mounted the stairs, moving slowly and examining every step. Third from the top he found the loose one. The outer edge was rotting, the wood flaking with age, and had nearly come free from the nails intended to secure it. The plank rattled and tilted in his grip.

Stephen descended the stair. "It's there. Could have been the cause."

"But you're not sure," Gilbert said shrewdly.

Stephen avoided his gaze and shrugged. He had ample reason for wanting more proof, since just last month he had mistaken murder for an accident, a lapse that had led to another man's death.

The man sent to fetch Mistress Webbere had returned with a woman of about thirty-five. She had a strong rather than pretty face, with the sort of broad jaw that would have looked well on a man but looked less well on a woman.

"You're Mistress Webbere?" Stephen asked.

"I am." Mistress Webbere spoke firmly in a high feminine voice that seemed odd coming from so masculine a face. It was a firm voice, used to command. "Your man tells me you wish to take . . . that into my house." She gestured to the body.

"Only for a short time. Until we've had a chance to examine him properly."

"I shall not allow it. It is unclean."

She had every right to refuse, although it surprised Stephen that she would not cooperate. He said, "Very well. William, Gilbert, could either of you arrange for a cart? We'll take Master Muryet to the castle. They'll have tables there they won't care about dirtying."

Mistress Webbere nodded firmly, a slight smile signaling her satisfaction.

Stephen gestured to the door at the top of the stairs. "What's up there?"

"A room."

"What kind of room?"

"She rents it out," Brandone said.

Stephen nodded. Trust the townsfolk to know the business of their neighbors. "To whom?" he asked.

"It's not rented now," Mistress Webbere said. Then she added hastily, "but it was last night. A woman took it in the evening, for one night only. She gave her name as Simone. She was a traveler in need of lodgings. My house is known in these parts as a place that gives a roof and a good bed to travelers at rates that are more affordable than other establishments." She cast a sly glance at Gilbert, as if in challenge to the Broken Shield, which posed her some competition.

Stephen exchanged glances with Gilbert. "And we are to believe that Muryet came to visit this lady traveler . . . just like that?"

"I do not inquire into the business of my tenants," Mistress Webbere said stiffly. "It is unseemly."

"You neither heard nor saw this Simone leave?"

"I did not," Mistress Webbere said firmly.

The man who had fetched Mistress Webbere had returned with a small cart. Stephen saw it arrive and said, "Well, I suppose there isn't much more we can do here. Let's get him loaded and on his way."

He picked four men from the crowd to lift the body to the cart. They moved with obvious reluctance, for no one could relish this chore, although it was necessary. And once the body was in the cart, it was disturbing to see it there, rigidly upright as if leaning against an invisible wall, the head so completely and unnaturally turned around.

The cart's driver snapped the reins and clicked his tongue. The cart horse started forward and the cart gave a jerk, rocking the body as it rattled down Corve Street toward town.

Stephen and Gilbert fell in behind the cart. A number of noisy small boys tailed after them for the enjoyment of the spectacle until Stephen turned on them with a scowl and a wave of the hand, which caused them to scatter like a flock of frightened doves. Warily, they reconvened further away, where they kept cautious pace behind the cart, laughing and chattering at a safer distance.

"It really could be an accident, you know," Gilbert said when some measure of peace and isolation had settled on the solemn little procession. "This Simone could have been a lover with whom he had an assignation last night."

"If it was an assignation, it was a secret one," Stephen said.

"And he fell down the steps in the dark upon taking his leave."

"I suppose."

"But you don't think so."

"How could a fall down a flight of steps turn a man's head around like that?"

"I don't know," Gilbert said. "I really don't know. I don't suppose there's no reason it could not, though. I've seen men with broken necks before. They weren't much different than that."

"And look there." Stephen pointed to Muryet's dagger sheath, which the dead man had carried in an unconventional fashion, thrust into his belt across his stomach, tilting toward the right, so he could make a right-handed draw. "The sheath of his dagger is empty. How could a fall make his dagger disappear?"

Chapter 3

The steward at the castle was no more anxious to have a contorted dead man displayed on a table in his hall than Mistress Webbere. After some delay, the coroner's party was diverted to the jail, which stood against the castle's outer wall near the main gate. No one at the castle wanted to have anything to do with touching the body, although there was no shortage here of gawkers any more than there had been in Corve Street. So it fell to Gilbert and the carter to manhandle the corpse through the narrow door into the cell provided.

The cell was a small dank room unfit even for horses which smelled so strongly of urine and feces and rotting straw that it made men want to gag. The carter did not waste any time fleeing from the horrid smell, leaving Stephen and Gilbert with the dead man, who lay on the floor in the shaft of light admitted by the open door, since there was no table. Stephen wished he could have fled too. It would have been better to conduct the examination in the well-lighted outer bailey, but he couldn't bear to do it in front of the eyes of the small crowd which had gathered at the door. He went to the doorway and stood with crossed arms. "Get on," he demanded. "Don't you people have work to do?"

After a few hard looks and obvious disappointment, the crowd broke up. Stephen stood there until the last of them had turned away. Then he went back into the cell.

Gilbert knelt over the corpse, fingering the empty dagger sheath.

"Perhaps it came loose," Gilbert said, referring to the missing dagger. "They do that sometimes."

"They aren't supposed to. You know that," Stephen said.

"What do I know about weapons?" Gilbert said. He folded his hands across his round stomach and leaned against the wall. It looked as though he was waiting for dinner rather than something far less appetizing. "Not my line of work, brawling. I am a man of the intellect. "

Stephen tipped his own dagger, a foot of slender steel which he carried on his right hip, upside down while still in its scabbard. A gift from his grandfather, it had been so much a part of his person since he was twelve years old that he hardly noticed it was there, but was keenly aware of its absence. "See how tightly the leather grips the blade so it won't fall out? It's made for that very purpose — to enclose the blade like a fist. Muryet's is no different."

Gilbert sighed. "Well, it certainly seems hard to see how it could have fallen out." He brightened at a thought. "Someone could have stolen it."

It was, Stephen had to admit, a more likely possibility. Was he wrong? Was he leaping to conclusions again? He hated to be wrong. He said, "Well, get on with it."

"Get on with what?"

"Cutting his clothes off, of course. I'm not reporting this death an accident until I've had a look at every inch of him. This won't be like last time."

"It's your turn. I did it last time."

"And you're the clerk. You're supposed to do as I say."

"I'm also your landlord."

"Well, we're not at the inn, so you're not wearing your landlord hat now."

"I should start charging you rent, if this is how things are going to be."

"I'll tell my cousin. I believe there's some matter of a debt?" Gilbert and Edith owed Stephen's cousin, the earl of Shelburgh, some debt that they were repaying by giving him room and board, although it was perhaps the meanest room in the inn, an attic space that you'd normally expect to house the boy who mucked out the latrines. Stephen had just been glad to have somewhere to go that hadn't cost him anything, since he hadn't any money. He had never been clear on the nature of the debt.

Gilbert dug into his pouch for his knife, grumbling. "Can't believe you'd bring that up." He fingered the knife. It was the one that he used for various chores, including eating.

Stephen could tell he was reluctant to use his eating knife on the dead man, so he took out his own knife and snapped it open. "Here, use this."

"Very kind of you."

"Think nothing of it."

Gilbert put his knife away and knelt by the corpse. Taking Muryet's coat by the collar at the back of his neck — eerily just below the chin — and sawed through the fabric of coat and shirt down to the belt at the dead man's waist. The belt gave some resistence, but the knife was sharp and was soon through it. Because the dead man's arms were still stiff and unbendable, Gilbert had to cut through the sleeves too. Shortly, the man's clothes on his upper body were in shreds on the ground and Gilbert quickly sliced through the stockings. As much as he might demur from this chore, it was one he had often done. For years he had been Sir Geoffrey Randall's clerk, and now, at Sir Geoff's withdrawal from active service although he still held the office and its considerable emoluments, served Stephen. Or was supposed to. When he was done, he stood and gave back the knife. "You may examine, your honor," he said.

Stephen sank beside the now-naked body and examined it closely, starting at the head. He ruffled the hair, looking for wounds, and found none on the scalp. There were the ones already noted on the face and he passed quickly over them. He noted several bruises on the upper back about the shoulders, one on the ribs under the right arm and none on the buttocks or backs of the legs. He heaved the body on its back as if it was a piece of furniture. The front of the legs and pelvis were an odd bluish-red, marked by strange streaks that seemed to mimic the wrinkles that might have been left by clothing such as a broad whitish band that obviously had been left by the man's belt. Even the outline of the buckle was evident. There were no obvious bruises or suspicious marks of any kind except for a bruise on the right shin, but it looked old and healing.

Shadows cast upon the body made him look up. Brandone and the other jurymen stood about the doorway. Distaste showed upon their faces. Although they were well accustomed to the gruesome indignity of death, the sight of the contorted and naked body, part marble gray and part bluish-red, might be more than they were used to. Or maybe it was the stench of the jail.

"I've brought the rest of the fellows, sir," Brandone said. "I thought you might like to get the business done as soon as possible."

Stephen stood up and nodded. Sometimes inquests were held in formal places, under roofs and around tables with chairs and benches to sit on. Other times, he was learning, they were held quickly in the open air. The main thing was to get a consensus about what had happened. Stephen wished he had thought to have water fetched so he could wash his hands before they got started. It seemed unclean to touch anything after what he had just done.

No one was inclined to enter, so Stephen stepped outside into slanting sunlight that seemed more golden and fresh than usual. A little breeze washed away the gagging smell and stung his face. There was a rickety bench outside the door. Stephen sat down on it. Gilbert settled beside him and the men sank onto the grass without waiting for his permission. Although there was a considerable social gulf between them, like Gilbert they acted as if they weren't much aware of it. This might have rubbed other men wrong, but Stephen, poor as he was, had no inclination to stand on frail dignity and hollow pride.

"Have you found out anything new?" Stephen asked Brandone.

A dozen heads wagged.

"No one saw or heard anything?" Stephen said.

"Not a thing," Brandone said.

"I can't believe that a fall down those stairs wouldn't make enough noise to attract someone's attention," Stephen said. "Particularly in Mistress Webbere's house."

"Not if they were dead asleep," one man said.

"Or dead drunk," another added.

"Drunk?" Stephen turned toward the speaker, a heavy set man named Thomas, a tanner.

"Helen Webbere's been known to swill a bit more than her fair share, 'specially since her last husband died. Neighbors found her passed out in a ditch down from the White Staff last spring." The White Staff was an alehouse this side of Corve Bridge, which was just up the road from the Webbere house.

Brandone grimaced. "Lay off, Tom. That was just after her old man passed on. She hasn't had that much trouble with drink."

"Tommy's mad at her because she won't diddle him," a man in the back said.

That brought a laugh. Thomas' face got red. Stephen smiled. He reckoned the accusation must be true.

"Did you find a dagger anywhere about?" Stephen asked Brandone.

Brandone looked puzzled. He shook his head. "No, never saw a dagger. Why?"

"Muryet was carrying one, but it's missing. It's not in its scabbard. I thought it might have fallen out when he fell — if he fell."

"No," Brandone said slowly. "Somebody could have picked it up."

"Which means that the boy who found the body wasn't the first finder after all," Stephen said.

"Well," Brandone said, "if I stole from a dead man, I'd not say I'd been there."

"Fair enough," Stephen said.

"I'm for taking a vote," the red-faced Thomas said abruptly. "I've got work to do and we're wasting time here. It's obvious what happened."

There was a murmur of agreement.

"What did happen?" Stephen asked.

"He fell down the stairs and broke his damned fool neck," Thomas said. "That's what happened."

"But what was he doing up the stairs?" Stephen asked.

"Who knows and who cares?" Thomas said. "Meeting some trollop in secret, most likely. Webbere didn't give details about the room because she's been renting it to whores."

"Are you sure about that?"

Surprisingly, there were a few nods. If Thomas held some grudge against Helen Webbere, he wasn't the only one who had doubts about her character.

Stephen glanced for support at Gilbert, who looked up from his knitted fingers and shrugged slightly. He didn't sense that Gilbert agreed with Thomas, but he didn't disagree so strongly that he felt compelled to say anything. Besides, it wasn't Gilbert's place to voice his opinions at an inquest, only to take down the conclusion.

"Isn't it a bit odd," Stephen said slowly, "that the only marks of any real substance on his body were on his face? Shouldn't a fall down the stairs have left bruises all over him? And scrapes? Yet he had none that I could see."

"Doesn't seem odd to me," Thomas said. "Dead men don't bruise. That's nonsense."

There was a murmur of agreement. Stephen could fairly smell the impatience. They had already made up their minds. There was nothing he could say that would change them.

"All right, then," Stephen said with some reluctance. "All in favor of death by misadventure?"

The chorus of ayes was loud; from almost every mouth.

"Any nays?" Stephen said.

There was silence. If there were any dissenters who had held back before, they were not speaking up.

"Is there a verdict as to cause?"

"The loose step," Brandone said.

"Do we agree on that?" Stephen asked.

Heads nodded all around.

Stephen glanced at Gilbert, who did not meet his eye. Gilbert seemed inordinately interested in a thread that had come loose from his sleeve.

"How much for the step?" Stephen asked. It was the law that the value of the instrument causing the death had to be assessed as a fine to the king.

"Aw," Thomas said, "I wouldn't give an eighth of a penny for it."

"What about the nails?" Stephen said with a slight smile. "Make it a quarter penny." Like it or not, it was his duty to try to persuade the jury to make the fine as large as possible.

"Weren't the nails' fault," Thomas said. "The board was plain rotten, and that's the end of it."

That was the end of the discussion. The deodand would be no more than an eighth of a penny. Stephen could hear Walter Henle's snort at such a ridiculous fine. But the assessment was the duty of the jury, and they were often lenient.

With no more business to conduct, the jurymen rose and hurried through the castle gate back to their shops. There were still hours of light left, and no one wanted to waste any more time.

Stephen and Gilbert remained on the bench. Although the air had a snap to it, the breeze had died, the sunlight was warm, and it was pleasant. Stephen felt heavy and didn't want to move.

"Why won't people see sense?" Stephen asked.

"It's a small town," Gilbert sighed. "People don't like to think that their neighbors would do murder. Besides, Muryet was unpopular. Some might secretly think he deserved what he got, and so aren't in a mood to point fingers."

"So you agree? It was not an accident?"

Gilbert was quiet for a time. "I said before, I don't know."

Stephen had a sharp retort on the tip of his tongue but it died there, killed by the sight of a party of horsemen who had just passed through the narrow main gate of the castle. Gilbert saw his startled expression and turned to see what had captured Stephen's attention.

"I'll be damned," Gilbert murmured. "No wonder the jail was empty. And to imagine I never gave it a thought."

At the head of the party rode Ademar de Valence, the king's justice, his fox-trimmed robe billowing about his twig-like legs. Behind rode Clement, the deceased Ancelin Baynard's former bailiff, who by rights should have been in the cell where Muryet lay, awaiting trial and execution for murder.

But that was not all.

"I hadn't heard that Clement had a son," Gilbert said, for Clement held a small child, a black-haired boy of no more than two, in his arms. When Clement's eyes fell on Stephen there on the bench, they lighted up and a nasty smile creased his square face.

"He isn't Clement's son," Stephen said. "He's mine."

Chapter 4

Ademar de Valence poised the child on his lap. He gazed over the boy's dark head to Stephen Attebrook, who sat on the edge of his chair opposite the judge. It took every ounce of Stephen's self-control to appear unconcerned and not to rush across the gap and seize Christopher. For a moment, he seriously considered taking action. He might actually manage to get away in the public commotion it would cause here in the castle's great hall, which was busy with people — a circle of ladies holding their sewing circle a short distance away before the great hearth; a group of merchants from the town who had come with some petition for Henle, the sheriff's representative; a swirl of young boys playing tag in a far corner; and servants setting up the tables for dinner. But he abandoned the idea. Clement was close by, as were more than half a dozen soldiers, who were lounging around as if they had nothing better to do. They would surely intervene if Stephen put up a struggle and he couldn't fight them all. Valence had him in his grip again after so many years, and Stephen felt as helpless in Valence's presence as he had as a boy.

Valence smiled. He couldn't help looking smug and self-satisfied. He patted the child's head with false affection, absently, as one would pat a dog.

Christopher, who never sat still for long, began to squirm, eager to be down on the floor. Valence motioned for Clement to take the boy. Clement was no more eager to hold him than Valence had been, and passed him off to his nurse, Gunnora. She knew how to deal with children if Valence and Clement did not. She grasped Christopher firmly by the hand and led him outside. Stephen forced himself not to watch them go.

"Have you been well, Stephen?" Valence said with studied laziness.

"Yes, your honor."

"Good, good," Valence said in a tone that indicated he didn't care. "What, may I ask, were you doing in the jail?"

"Investigating a death."

"Oh? Whose?"

"William Muryet's."

Valence frowned at the mention of the name. Stephen had the distinct impression Valence had heard it before, but just in case he had not Stephen added, "He was the butler to Olivia Baynard, Anselin Baynard's widow."

"I know that," Valence said testily. He hated giving the impression of not knowing things or being reminded of things he already knew. "What happened?"

"The jury think he got drunk and fell down a flight of stairs and broke his neck."

"Odd," Valence said. "So odd." Then he said briskly, "Such a distasteful little man. He won't be missed, I'm sure."

"What's odd about his death?"

"Well, it is the merest coincidence," Valence replied, steepling his long, beringed fingers. "But it seems that something important has gone missing from the Baynard House — something of great importance to the crown."

Stephen suddenly felt chillier than warranted by the drafts ever present in the hall. "What would that be?"

"Stephen, you have many faults, but sheer stupidity is not among them. I think you know."

Stephen glanced at Clement, who was gazing hard into the fire, which had burned low on the hearth in the center of the hall and needed another log. "I'm not your apprentice any more, and I won't play your guessing games. You want something. What is it?"

Valence clutched the arms of the chair and leaned forward, eyes flashing. When he got angry like this, Stephen and his fellow apprentice James de Kerseye had joked that his eyes would pop out of his head. But his eyes did not pop out; the glare receded. Valence said with dangerous calm, "I see. To confess knowledge is to confess your own theft. That's understandable. Well, let me just say this. There was a certain document among Baynard's things, a list of names and accounts. This list has disappeared. I want it back. It seems you've developed a skill at ferreting out secrets. I want you to ferret this one. I know you've seen it, so you won't be duped by some forgery. Get me that list."

Stephen's chill deepened. "What if it can't be got?"

"I am certain you will exhaust every avenue of inquiry. You'll find it." Valence paused then said, "In the meantime, I have taken your son under my protection."

"He was fine where he was."

"With all due respect to your cousin the earl, the boy will turn into a country bumpkin like yourself if he remains at Shelburgh. You can't actually imagine that Eustace really would lavish money or attention on your bastard, can you? Bastards always get the crumbs and the bastards of poor relatives get the smallest crumbs of all. In my household, he will have access to the best that English society has to offer. If I have your cooperation, of course."

"Naturally."

"Good, then. We understand each other. Well, don't just sit there. Get to work! Time is wasting."

When Stephen had left the hall, Clement fetched a cup of wine for Valence. He knelt as he handed the cup and leaned close. The hall was crowded and he did not want to be overheard.

"My lord," said Clement, "would you really bring up the pup almost as if he was your son?"

Valence accepted the cup and swirled the contents, as if he was an alchemist inspecting his brew. "I am a firm believer that rewards are more effective than punishments in motivating men." He fixed his eyes on Clement. "Including men such as yourself."

"Yes, my lord."

Valence sipped his wine. "Besides, I'll be spared the expense in the end. When he's done his little chore, he will demand the boy back. He has this grudge against me, you see. He was a wild ungovernable boy with a passionate nature. When, as was my duty, I tried to impose a small measure of discipline, he rebelled. As you could see on his face he has not forgotten what passed between us. So I shall give the odious child up — a small price to pay for so valuable a thing, don't you think?"

"What if he fails?"

"Ah, now there is a rub. How can I punish him? For after all, one must punish failure in some way. What shall I do?"

"You could give the child to me."

Valence smiled thinly. "Don't imagine I haven't thought of that."

"It never occurred to me you had not, my lord."

"You'd like that, wouldn't you."

"Yes, my lord."

"We shall see, Clement. We shall see." He added, "You would take good care of him, if I did?"

"Of course, my lord."

"I'm glad to hear that."

Clement added probingly, "But still, my lord, children die all the time. Fevers and fluxes and such. Accidents."

"It would be a pity."

Clement nodded solemnly. "It would, sir."

Valence smiled. "I knew you would be useful, Clement. As I've said, show me loyalty and you will go far. We shall have much work to do."

"I'm your man, my lord. I said so."

"Good, good."

Stephen was trembling when he emerged from the great hall. Gilbert was waiting for him by the gate to the outer bailey, which ran through the base of the castle's inner wall beside the old keep, a great square tower. Stephen struggled to get himself under control as he crossed the inner bailey. The look on his face caused Gilbert to be alarmed.

"What happened in there?" Gilbert asked anxiously as he hurried through the gate after Stephen. Stephen's legs were so much longer than his and his pace so rapid that Gilbert had to jog to keep up. If Stephen wasn't so angry, he'd have thought the sight was comical. Few things were as amusing as Gilbert running, unless it was Gilbert trying to ride a mule.

"Baynard's list is missing," Stephen spat. "Valence wants me to find it. He holds Christopher as a hostage for my good behavior."

"Oh, dear."

"My bastard of a cousin. He gave Christopher over." Stephen wasn't sure what angered him more at this instant: his cousin's betrayal or Valence's veiled threat. He hadn't actually promised to harm Christopher, but the threat had been here, if he failed. He had sensed it like a rotten smell.

"Your cousin?"

"I returned from Spain after —" Stephen's voice faltered ever so slightly. He almost mentioned the death of the boy's mother, Taresa, but he had never spoken of that to anyone in England. The pain of her loss was so great he could barely think her name, let alone say it aloud. "— to place my boy with Eustace. I don't have the means to raise him, and I wanted him to have a start in life, I wanted him raised English in my family, not on the streets of some miserable Spanish town. Eustace promised to take care of him."

"Perhaps Eustace didn't have a choice. Valence is a powerful man with powerful friends."

"So he is," Stephen snarled. "But that's no reason to betray family. Family comes first, or it's supposed to."

"Politics, it's politics," Gilbert said, gasping for breath. "Politics and money often trump family loyalty. I say, would you mind slowing down? I can hardly keep up."

Stephen stopped so abruptly that Gilbert had to put out his hands to keep from running into him.

"That better?" Stephen said.

Gilbert panted, "Thanks so much. I haven't run so far since I was a boy. I thought my heart would stop."

They were more than halfway across the vast outer bailey. The jail, with its gaping door, lay no more than forty yards away. Gilbert saw Stephen looking at it. For a moment they both stared at the open door. A whitish object was just visible there, a portion of Muryet's corpse.

"Muryet," Stephen said grimly. "I'll wager whoever killed him did so over the list. We find Muryet's killer and we find the list."

Gilbert looked skeptical. "Stephen, let's not be hasty. Even if it was murder — a long if — it could simply be a coincidence."

"Do you really believe that?"

"I don't know. The world is full of mysteries. Not all are capable of solution." Gilbert sighed and scuffed the ground with his toe. He looked up and squinted against the sun. "All right. I'll take your wager. A kettle of Edith's mutton pie."

"Done." Stephen grinned without humor and stepped lively toward the main gate. "And don't go thinking I'll share any of it with you, either."

Chapter 5

Saturday the twenty-first dawned cold and rainy. A light drizzle filtered from gray clouds that pressed down on the hilltop town like the palm of God's hand. Stephen, who normally threw open the shutters first thing, parted them only a crack, and shivered with the chill wet wind that hissed through that little space while he took his bath from the bowl by the window. He washed his face and hands, arms and legs, chest and back, with the soapy rag, rinsed, and toweled off. By the time he was done, his teeth were chattering. He had only been back in England about two months and after nine years in Spain, he wasn't used to the cold. He figured he would get his fill of English chill this coming winter. He was glad to be home, but not for the weather.

He turned from the window and struggled quickly into his clothes: linen undershirt and drawers, woolen tunic, and wool breeches. They were made of thick English wool raised right outside town and woven here on a loom whose home he could have seen if he opened the shutters only a little wider. He felt better now. He wished people in England had some means of heating their houses better, or that he had a fireplace. But this was a servant's room, tucked into the top floor at the back of the house, and did not rate such a luxury.

Properly armored against the English autumn, he let one shutter open and perched on the sill to think. He liked the scene that lay below the window. The inn lay about halfway up the ridge that formed the backbone of the town, and from this height, he had a good view of the southern part of Ludlow. Its houses ran down the hillside, peaked rooftop after rooftop, to the River Teme, just visible over the town wall. On the other side of the river, lay the suburb of Ludford, the tower of its little parish church cloaked in a rainy mist surrounded by its screen of elms, which had lost all their leaves. The countryside beyond was a patchwork of greens, yellows, and browns. Although today, there was something odd about the tableau. He could not put his finger on exactly what it was. Something was out of order; something not quite right.

It was a melancholy morning, the sort of morning where you'd like to draw near the fire with your ale pot on your knee, if like Stephen you had no regular job to do. He did not want to go out in this wet, but he had to. He had to do something. There was no point in wasting the day. The thought of Christopher in Valence's grip was too infuriating and frightening to sit around swilling ale and feeling sorry for himself. The problem was, he had no idea what to do. Although he firmly believed that all the signs pointed to murder in Muryet's death, there was nothing that indicated who had done it or why. Despite his confident wager with Gilbert, he knew nothing that clearly pointed to Muryet's involvement in the disappearance of the list. All he had was hasty supposition and inference.

"I should have taken it when I had the chance," he said to himself. A month ago, he had been in Baynard's library and had seen — even held — the list. It was two lists, actually, one of the king's informers and agents and a second of those whom Baynard had identified as Montfort's supporters, informers, and agents. He had broken into Baynard's writing box to find something else entirely, an anonymous note that had lured Ancelin Baynard to his death from ambush just across the street from the Broken Shield. He had taken the note, and left the list. He had not wanted any part of the fight between the king and his corrupt supporters and the reformers. In fact, in his heart, he thought, from what little he knew about the dispute, that the reformers had the better argument. But he still didn't want to take sides. He just wanted to live his life undisturbed, to savor his grief unmolested. Taresa's death had left a yawning hole in his spirit. There was no room for the petty controversies of men.

Beneath him, the inn was stirring. He heard voices in conversation. The old wooden structure creaked and thumped as guests awoke, made their toilets, dressed, and clattered down to the hall, where Edith and Jennie would be setting out breakfast. If he didn't go now, there'd likely be nothing left. So he pulled on his boots, stuffing a rag in the toe of the left one to take the place of his missing toes. Ducking to avoid the slanting beams of the roof, which he knew from experience could give the unwary a nasty knock on the head, he made his way across the room to the door. As an afterthought, without any consideration where he might go, he took his old blue woolen cloak from its peg, draped it over his arm and stepped out into the corridor.

The hall swirled with activity in the warm yellow light of the fire raging in the fireplace and candles placed in strategic spots in little cradles attached to posts. Although breakfast was a light meal, typically bread and cheese and left over cold meat when it was available, it was always well attended at the Shield. There must have been more than twenty people crammed into the hall, devouring the loaves and half-rounds of cheese that Jennie and Nan, another of the servant girls, scurried to pass out. Other guests were taking their leave and settling their bills at the door, where Edith presided over the coin box and scales for weighing money with the aplomb of a bishop counting his offerings. She knew what every person owed to the penny without having to write a single thing down; God knew how she kept it all straight. Gilbert was not in sight, although it was not his habit to sleep late.

Almost every space at the trestle tables was taken, even Stephen's favorite spot between the stairway and the fire. This meant there was nowhere to sit without elbowing someone aside, and he didn't feel up to that indignity. His pride, feeble as it was, imposed some limits, and jostling with tavern guests for space at a table was beyond them. So he intercepted a fragment of a loaf as one guest prepared to pass it to another, and scooped a half-round of cheese from Jennie's tray as she wended her way from the larder in the rear of the building to a front table. She looked at him with mock indignation and waited until he had broken off a large piece of cheese. When he returned the half-round to her tray, she gave him a smile and moved to the waiting table, swaying her ample hips perhaps more than she should have. Certainly, her mother would not have approved had she seen it.

The door to the street was jammed, so Stephen slipped out the door to the yard. The yard held its usual bustle of early morning activity. One of the menservants was stoking the fire next to the orchard which would double for brewing ale and laundry, a boy was staggering under a load of wood for the fireplace indoors, Nan came out with a basket of dirty linens, and the door to the stables stood open and a guest's groom was leading a pair of saddled horses into the light.

And Stephen realized what had struck him as out of sorts before.

When he had looked down at the yard, the stable doors had been closed.

Normally, Harry opened them with the crowing of the cocks. It took him a long time to crawl on his hands from his bed in the stables to his licensed begging spot at Broad Gate, and he liked to get an early start so he could be on station for the morning traffic. He worked his spot even in the rain because the gate warden let him shelter under the gate arch.

The fact the door had been closed meant Harry had not gone out. And that meant something was wrong with him.

Stephen crossed the yard to the stable and went in. The windows were all shut against the rain, and it was dark and gloomy. A wet cough sounded from the left. Horses snickered. A few stuck their heads out to look at him, perhaps anxious to be fed. Stephen had to wait a moment for his eyes to adjust, then he went left. Harry lived in the last stall. Stephen paused at the door to the stall. It was smaller than all the others and was used for storing hay. On the left side, bales were piled to the ceiling. At the right corner, Harry lay curled on a nest of hay beneath a wool blanket. He had driven pegs in the wall about three feet from the ground. His floppy wool hat, a spare shirt, and a ratty cloak hung from the pegs. The thick padded leather gloves that he wore to protect his hands were hooked over the spare shirt.

"You out carousing late last night and get caught in the wet?" Stephen asked.

Harry coughed wetly. He spat a wad of mucus and said a dirty word. "No. I was in at my proper bedtime, and tucked away like the wee child I am. You, on the other hand, fell asleep with a candle burning. Saw the light in your window. Shame on you. Trying to kill our hosts, are you?"

"I didn't leave it burning. I couldn't sleep."

"The weight of all that sin you're carrying?" Harry coughed again, and panted to catch his breath, which came in wheezy gasps.

"Sin? Man, I am guiltless."

"Guiltlessness and sinless aren't necessarily the same thing. The one means you just don't feel the sin, though it's there. Anyway, I think you're lying. You may not be among the churchgoing, but you're too honest not to feel your burden."

"What do you know about William Muryet?" Stephen asked to change the subject.

Harry cocked an eye at him. "Muryet? He's the one found dead yesterday. Broken neck, I heard."

"That's right."

"Fell down a flight of stairs visiting a trollop at Webbere's place."

"Maybe."

"Can't say as I'm sorry." He hitched his blanket higher on his shoulders. Stephen noticed that he was shivering. Harry said, "You looking to indict someone with this one too?"

"I thought I might."

Harry chuckled. "You'll probably have to indict half the town."

"Brandone said something like that."

"Yeah, he would, and he's one of those at the front of the line."

"Why do you say that?"

"Muryet, he was too free and easy with the dice, you know. He liked them as much as some men like their women.

Used to kiss them before he threw. But they didn't like him. He lost a lot. Left notes all over town. Brandone's holding one. Thomas Tanner's another he owed money."

"Gilbert said he and Edith were owed too."

"Oh, yeah. I forgot about them. They let him run a bill, the fools. I thought Edith had more sense. You're about the only person in Ludlow Muryet didn't owe money to, and that's only because you haven't been here long enough."

"So how much money did he owe you?"

Harry snorted. "I'm not a gambling man. What would I have to gamble with?"

"You lie."

"If I wasn't so short, I'd cut your heart out."

"You've wagered with me."

"That's different."

"What do you mean?"

"Because I know if I won, you'd pay up. Muryet? What good's a note to me? I can't read. He could have put anything on it — a nursery rhyme, dirty words. Have you ever seen filthy words written down?"

Stephen shook his head.

"Wonder what they look like." Harry was wracked by a spasm of coughing. When he finally stopped he said, "There's one thing odd about all this, though."

"What?"

"I heard that Webbere wasn't renting her room to a trollop. At least not a trollop that Muryet was visiting."

"What do you mean?"

"Well, I heard from a lass who's a string maker for William Brandone that the room was let to a countrywoman who holds two hides in the west."

"How would she know that?"

"The woman bought from her, that's why. To make her own candles."

"Imagine, remembering such a thing."

"Well, you'd remember it too if you lived next door and saw the man coming and going late at night."

"Who's to say it wasn't Muryet?"

"The lass said it was a big burly fellow. Muryet's the size of a bantam cock."

"Any idea who the visitor was?"

"Sure."

"Who then?"

"Don't know as I'll tell you. I don't want to ruin anyone's reputation. I'm not a gossipmonger."

"Could have fooled me. You've got looser lips than most fishwives."

"You're so free with flattery. It turns my heart. Bet your lack of charm is the reason why you haven't got a woman."

That stung a bit, but Stephen let it pass. Stephen noticed that Harry's eyes were fixed on the cheese in his hands. Slowly, he raised the lump and took a bite. Harry's eyes followed the progress of the lump up and down. "Hungry, Harry?"

"No."

"Didn't think so."

"A man doesn't need but one good meal a day. You'll get gouty, like Sir Geoff, if you keep eating so much."

"Who was the man, Harry?"

Harry's need got the better of his self-control. He held out his hand. Stephen gave him the cheese.

"The bread, too," Harry said.

"I'm not sure this is worth it."

"You'll never know until you pay."

Stephen gave him the bread. When their hands brushed, Stephen thought Harry's arm was unnaturally warm. He touched Harry's face with the back of his hand. Now he was sure Harry was running a fever. Harry threw off the hand.

"Leave off, you bastard," Harry said. "I didn't give you permission to touch me."

"Sorry, Harry," Stephen said.

There were a few moments of silence while Harry enjoyed his fee.

"Well?" Stephen said. "Who was he?"

Harry chewed and swallowed loudly. "A fellow I think you know, which is remarkable, since you have so few friends. Name of Howard Makepeese. Worked for Baynard as a groom, or something like that."

Stephen stood up. He indeed remembered Howard Makepeese.

Harry asked anxiously, "You won't tell anyone how I heard about this, will you? About the string lass, I mean. If it got out that she was selling on the side, Brandone will discharge her."

"Don't worry, Harry. I won't say a word to anyone."

Chapter 6

Jennie scowled at Stephen when he returned to the inn. She snatched up a broom which had been hanging from a leather strap on a post. "You're supposed to wipe your feet when you come in," she snapped. "Why can't you men remember something so simple?"

Stephen blinked, taken aback. She had never spoken sharply like this to him. It was amazing how much like her mother she looked and sounded when she lost her temper. He glanced back at the way he'd come. His tracks were clearly visible on the well-swept wood floor. So, he'd made extra work for her. She was angry because if she didn't clean up the mess, she'd feel the edge of Edith's tongue, something nobody enjoyed.

He said, "Listen, Harry's running a fever. It's bad enough that he hasn't gone out to work this morning. Could you see that he gets a bowl of hot broth later?" He gave her a quarter penny. "And don't tell him it came from me, all right?"

Now it was Jennie's turn to be surprised. Her fingers curled over the shard of coin. "Sure, I will."

Stephen gave her his best smile and her own blossomed in return. He touched the brim of his hat as if she was the finest lady, which made her redden, and beat a quick retreat through the front door to Bell Lane before she had a chance to remember how much he'd dirtied up the floor.

A misty rain still fell, pricking Stephen's cheeks, as he emerged onto Bell Lane. A few of the shops on the street had their shutters down in hopes of attracting a few customers. The shoemaker across the way could be seen sewing leather, his apprentice looking over his shoulder. The spoon and knife-maker next door had only one shutter down and voices there were raised in argument. It sounded like the wife was getting the best of it. Smoke billowed from the chimney of the glass-maker's just beyond Mistress Bartelot's house, and as Stephen passed the master turned from his furnace and waved in greeting. But the hopes of industry were frustrated this morning. The lane was deserted. Apart from Stephen, the only person in view was a boy Stephen recognized as one of the town pickpockets, who was sheltering against the side of a house at the corner with Broad Street. Stephen hardly gave the boy a glance.

Broad Street was as empty as Bell Lane. A rivulet was struggling to form in the center of the street. When it rained heavily, people called the street Broad Stream. During storms, the rivulet could grow to a sizeable flow. Stephen had heard stories since he was a boy about people trying to jump the stream when it was in flood and being carried all the way down the hill to Broad Gate. He had never known that actually to happen to anyone, but it was a standing joke.

The street at the top of the hill was not so deserted. There were several carts trundling along, turning the moist dirt of the street into Ludlow's well known mud. Far down the street, a small party of horsemen was disappearing single file through the castle gate. One of the town's matrons bustled by, the veil of her wimple billowing behind her. Three servant girls hustled to keep up. The matron nodded a curt good day to Stephen, for as a crown official he could not politely be ignored, although the severe cast of her eye suggested she would have liked to pretend he wasn't there. He bowed courteously in return, although as the wife of a tradesman she did not rate it. Sir Geoff had warned that the job demanded keeping on good terms with the town's leading citizens, and that required flattering their wives. The girls looked at him and giggled. One of them winked and blew him a kiss. She was young and pretty and obviously unattached. He accepted the gesture with a smile, a spasm of desire, and a pang of regret. He wondered what her name was. But there wasn't time or opportunity to speak to any of them.

With a sigh, he turned away toward College Lane, the narrow passage that ran north from High Street to the wall. As he passed St. Laurence's parish church, a schoolboy who was obviously late dashed passed him and through the churchyard gate. The schoolmaster met the boy at the school door with a clout on the head.

The house he sought lay at the end of the lane by the little gate in the wall. Master Baynard had been a rich man. He had held three houses in the town. Two of them had been used as shops, their living quarters rented out to journeymen, and he had lived in this one. Now he was dead, and his widow, Olivia Baynard, occupied it as her dower portion.

Stephen reached Baynard House just as a travelers' party rode through Linney Gate. Stephen was surprised to see Olivia Baynard at the head of the party. She was a plain-looking woman with an overlarge nose that gave her profile an unbalanced appearance. But she offset her physical deficiencies with a fine maroon gown embroidered with gold, which her traveling cloak did nothing to hide. She ignored him, turning her horse to ride through the gate to the yard of the house, followed by a retinue of grooms. But Stephen's eyes did not linger on Olivia Baynard. They were drawn to the woman beside her: she was well, but modestly dressed in a dark green gown under a dark red cloak. The hood was up but did not conceal her face. She was one of the most beautiful women he had ever seen: skin white as alabaster, a heart-shaped face, cool eyes under thin blonde brows, a tiny nose and bud of a mouth. The entire effect was saintly and almost childlike in its sweetness. That green gown and cloak draped elegantly over her breasts and body suggested concealed carnal treasures. Slender, ungloved fingers held the horse's reins with easy familiarity. Unlike Mistress Baynard, this woman looked frankly, though coolly, at Stephen. He felt a blush seep into his cheeks. Then, fortunately, the party passed out of sight into the yard.

Stephen waited an interval while he caught his breath. Then he knocked on the door.

A maid answered. "Your business, sir?" she asked with the right degree of cool respect.

"I've come to speak with Howard Makepeese," Stephen said.

That was not an answer she had expected. Gentry — because Stephen was obviously of the gentry by his clothes, although they were a bit shabby, and his accent — did not normally ask about servants. Her mouth fell open. But she recovered quickly. "He is no longer employed here, sir," she said primly. "You shall have to inquire elsewhere."

Stephen was disappointed. He had expected this to be easy. "And where would I inquire?"

"I have no idea, sir," the maid said tartly. "I do not make it a habit of marking Howard Makepeese's comings and goings, or to take account of his business, if it can be called that."

Stephen smiled. "You do not approve of Makepeese?"

"He is trouble, sir. He was trouble when he was here, and I've no doubt he is trouble where he is now."

"Trouble to whom?" Stephen asked.

"To young women, sir. He is a dog, a liar and untrustworthy."

She said this with such heat that Stephen suspected that she was one Makepeese had lied to in his career. It sounded like the usual story. A man will do and say anything to charm a woman, and the woman, wanting to be charmed, will believe the lies. When the man has what he wants, on he goes, leaving the woman feeling used, soiled, hurt and bewildered, and unpregnant if she was lucky. The maid then added, "And he is a ruffian." There was a pause and she went on in a much lower voice with a glance backward to see if she could be overheard. "Master Clement brought him into the house, if you know what I mean."

Stephen had a strong suspicion what she meant. "He knocked heads for Clement?"

The maid nodded. "Although it was on the master's orders. Most of the time, anyway. Their secret business. I'm told you know about that."

"Yes. I had heard about it."

They were interrupted by a woman calling from the hall. Even though she must have been some distance back in the house, the voice carried the snap of command. "Lucy, what in the devil's name are you doing? Close that door!"

Lucy disappeared behind the door. "It's a caller, mistress."

"Well, either send him on his way or let him in. You're letting in the cold."

"Sorry, mistress. It's the deputy coroner, mistress."

A conversation followed that was too low for Stephen to make out. Then the door swung open and Lucy, the maid, stepped aside to admit him. "The mistress bids you enter," she said.

"Thank you, Lucy," Stephen said.

She led him past the front rooms to the hall. Olivia Baynard was removing her calfskin gloves before the great fireplace at the far end. It was obvious she had just come in from the wet. A boy was depositing an armload of firewood and a manservant was stoking the fire to liven it up. Stephen couldn't help looking again at Olivia's companion. She faced the fire and he saw only her profile. She seemed so young, so gentle, so sweet, so in need of protection. He could look at that innocent face for hours and not grow bored with it.

But Olivia Baynard would not allow that. "Sir Stephen," she said. "My apologies. I did not recognize you when we came in, otherwise I'd not have allowed you to linger in the street."

Stephen jerked his attention from the companion. Olivia surprised him by speaking in French. He had not expected that. It signaled that she was not from the merchant class, but from the gentry, and she wanted him to know it. He replied in the same language. "No harm done. Lucy kindly told me what I needed to know."

"She says you're looking for Howard Makepeese."

"Yes."

"Does it have anything to do with poor William's death?"

"I'm afraid it does."

"You don't think . . . they said it was an accident."

"The jury think it was an accident. I'm not satisfied of that yet."

"Oh, dear." Olivia shuddered. Stephen noticed for the first time how delicate she seemed, how slender and swanlike. Stephen's first impression of Olivia had been that she was not an attractive woman, but there was something deliciously sensual in the way she moved and carried herself. He also noticed that she was barely in her twenties, much younger than her deceased husband. Youth and that swanish elegance must have been what drew Baynard to her; because she was gentry, she had married down, and probably had brought no property to the marriage. A rich man like Baynard could afford to marry for love or lust. Olivia grinned ruefully and said, "If anyone's capable of murder it's Howard. But I can't see Howard doing violence to William. They were the best of friends — odd friends, but good friends."

"Odd? Odd in what way?"

"Oh, that is a delicate matter," Olivia said, glancing at the companion.

The companion turned from the fire at this. "Oh, come now, Olivia. Since when have you ever shrunk from speaking the truth in front of me." She spoke to Stephen now, even though they had not yet been introduced. "Olivia and I are childhood friends. We shared every secret once."

Olivia suddenly realized she had forgotten her manners. "Sir Stephen, may I present my good dear friend, Lady Margaret de Thottenham. She has just come this very hour to comfort me in my bereavement. She has experience in widowhood, being a widow herself."

"My pleasure, Lady Margaret," Stephen said. She looked him straight in the eye in a way that was not at all demure and ladylike. They were blue eyes, he noticed, as blue as the sky, and frank and penetrating and watchful, and yet there was something playful about them as well. Those eyes, and the rest of her, were enough to make even a king's heart beat faster. For his certainly had started to wrack distressingly. He had to remind himself that she stood much higher on the social scale than he did and he would have to be careful about revealing his feelings for fear of giving offense.

He said, "Mistress Baynard, what was odd about their friendship?"

"Well," Olivia shrugged, "William was the sort of man who cared more for men than for women, if you know what I mean — and Howard cares for women far too much for anyone's good. Yet they seemed to like each other inordinately."

Margaret looked stunned. Clearly, she came from a sheltered country background. "You can't mean he was a —"

Olivia nodded gravely. "I'm afraid so."

"And you allowed him in your house!" Margaret gasped. Homosexuals were considered evil by most people; some churchmen even preached they were spawn of the devil and dealing with them could lead to damnation. As if in surprise, she touched his arm, but withdrew her hand as she realized the social mistake she had just made. She whispered, "Oh, dear."

"Ancelin found him useful," Olivia said defensively. "And he was. He was very efficient."

"You don't suspect there was anything . . . untoward between them?" Stephen asked. He did not want to offend Margaret, who seemed shocked. He had this strong impulse to protect her, to shelter her from the harsh realities of the world. But he had to know.

"No," Olivia said with conviction. "I do not. I'd have heard of it, surely. You can't keep secrets like that in a household."

Stephen had leapt to the suspicion that Muryet had died as a result of a lover's quarrel: he had discovered that Howard had a woman on the side, had jealously confronted him, and been killed for his trouble. Olivia's firmness in the matter made that possibility seem remote. But that didn't let Makepeese off the hook. Any number of other reasons could disrupt the best friendship and lead to murder.

Stephen said carefully, "Men of William's persuasion rarely fail to form attachments with other men. Do you know of anyone who might have been . . ."

Olivia looked distressed and glanced at Margaret, then shook her head. "I have no direct knowledge of his . . . activities, but he spent a great deal of time at a bathhouse. Indeed, he and Howard often went there together. The one by the river across from St. John's Hospital. I suspect you'll find the answer to that question there."

"Oh my," said Margaret.

Stephen nodded. Then he remembered why he had come. "Tell me about Makepeese. Why was he discharged?"

Olivia sniffed. "He was no longer needed. My husband's death . . . Clement's arrest . . ." she waved a delicate, long-fingered hand.

"Do you know where he's gone?"

"No idea. You may ask the staff, if you wish. But I doubt they have any more idea than I have. I hear all their talk and no one's said a word about him."

Stephen wondered just how true it was that she knew all the house gossip. As a child, Stephen had spent enough time eavesdropping on the staff to know that staff was able to conceal what it wished from the lords of a house. But Howard's whereabouts did not seem like anything they would care to hide. He didn't feel like ordering the assembly of the household staff to put this question to them. If anyone might know, he suspected it would be Lucy, and she'd known nothing. There were other places he could go for that information.

He glanced behind and above him at the door to Baynard's study. He gestured toward the door. "Who in the household has access to that room since Clement was arrested?"

Olivia's chin rose. "Why do you ask?" she said coldly.

"My lord Valence has directed me to enquire about a missing document."

Olivia sighed. "Apart from Clement, only William had permission to enter the room."

Stephen nodded. "I would like to see his rooms, if I may."

Olivia frowned and shrugged. "Very well." She turned and called in English to Lucy, who stood waiting by the fireplace, "Please take Sir Stephen to William's room."

Lucy bent a knee. "Yes, my lady."

Lucy led Stephen up the stairway beside the fireplace. Behind it he knew the house stretched far back from the street with an upper floor full of rooms. As he followed the maid down one of two corridors that ran to the rear of the house, he heard muffled laughter coming from the hall.

Olivia and Margaret fell into each other's arms. They laughed so hard that tears flowed down Margaret's cheeks. Olivia wiped them for her.

"What were you doing, you brat!" Olivia exclaimed between gasps.

"Hush!"

"Oh, tosh. He can't hear now." Olivia's laughter subsided to giggles. "I thought you might actually pretend to faint."

"At least you did not give me away."

"Why play the swan with the likes of him? It will encourage familiarity."

"I like him. I wouldn't mind if he came calling. You shall have to find a way to invite him for dinner."

Olivia was scandalized. "But he's practically a pauper. What would you want with a man like that?"

"He's rather handsome. And he seems decent. It's hard to find a decent man. You'll discover, Olivia, now you're a widow, that you've far more freedom to indulge yourself than you had before. If you find a man attractive, you can have him, and no one will question you, as long as he is of the right class and you are discrete. And I so need a good man. It's been so long."

"I have to warn you, Margaret, if you decide to pursue this thing, that he's deformed."

"How so?"

"His foot."

"I saw nothing wrong with it."

"There was that limp."

"It was hardly noticeable."

"They say a Moor chopped it off." Olivia made a chopping motion with one hand against the palm of the other.

"All of it?"

"No, it's said only part."

Margaret laughed. "As long as the best part of him works. He's presentable, he speaks nicely." Her expression became wistful. "We aren't allowed to marry for love, but who's to say we can't find it somehow?"

William had occupied a chamber on the south side of the house. It was dim inside. Stephen crossed the room as soon as he entered and opened the shutters of the sole window. Unlike the windows in the hall, it had no glass. It was still raining and a gust of wind caused Lucy to grip her arms and shiver. Stephen ignored the rain and the chill. At least now he could see.

The walls and ceiling were painted alternating stripes of blue and green. A large frame bed dominated the room. Its wooden frame, like the walls was painted blue and green stripes, which spiraled up the bedposts. Linen curtains had been pulled back and tied with blue ribbon. The bed was neatly made. It was covered with a woolen blanket of dark red. White linen pillows lined the top, waiting for an occupant who would be late. Stephen pushed on the mattress. It was soft and yielding. It felt like down, small feathers too. Very expensive.

"Did Muryet own the mattress?" Stephen asked.

Lucy frowned. "I think so, sir."

Stephen ran his eyes over the rest of the room. There was a wardrobe beside the door. Neatly folded clothes lay on its shelves. They weren't as colorful as the walls: mainly severe whites, browns and blacks. Stephen had met William before only twice briefly, and he remembered him as being very soberly dressed and rather dour in demeanor.

Beside the wardrobe was the customary chamber pot, empty of course, and in the corner by the door was a little table on which a small bronze cross stood, flanked by two unlighted candles. A small book lay at the base of the cross. It was odd to find a book here — as it had been to find books in Baynard's study. Books were expensive and only the wealthy had them. Stephen, who had a secret liking for books, idly opened it. It was written in Latin. He recognized it as the confessions of St. Augustine.

To his rear by the window where it could catch the light was a writing desk and a high-backed chair with a pillow on the seat. The writing desk had a shelf divided into little square compartments that reminded Stephen of a honeycomb. Each comb held rolled up documents. Stephen began pulling them out. They all dealt with household matters, mainly lists of supplies with prices, some accounts, and copies of a few letters, all written in a crabbed, barely legible hand. This was not surprising since the usual job of a butler was to manage the purchase of household supplies. There was no list of names, however. Not that Stephen had expected to find it in the comb. William would not have been so stupid as to hide the list there.

There was a box beside the shelves of the kind people used to store jewelry or coins. It had a little keyhole, but when Stephen prodded the lid, he found it was not locked. He opened the box. It was empty. The presence of the box suggested that Muryet had once had valuable goods or money. The fact it was empty suggested that he had sold the contents to pay his ubiquitous debts — yet he had evidently shrunk from selling his edition of St. Augustine. Curious, that.

Stephen pressed on the seat pillow, hoping to feel the crunch of a parchment concealed inside. But the pillow seemed to be filled only with wool stuffing.

He returned to the bed. He tore off the blanket and linen sheet and pulled the mattress onto the floor.

"Sir!" cried Lucy.

"What is it?" Stephen snapped, not looking at her. He was examining the fabric for signs of a cut and the seams for signs they had been re-stitched.

"N-n-nothing, sir," Lucy said.

"Huh," Stephen grunted.

Despite his hopes, nothing was concealed in the mattress.

He checked the pillows in the same meticulous way, but they too gave no sign of concealing any secrets.

After that, to Lucy's further astonishment, he crawled under the bed frame to look for secret compartments. He found none. He tapped on the walls and the wardrobe, hoping for a loose board or the tell-tale hollow sound of a hidden cupboard. But all he got was skinned knuckles.

Stephen straightened up and sucked on one of his knuckles. "Well," he said. "That was a waste of time."

"It certainly was," Lucy said, surveying the mess which she would have to clean up.

"I'll see Clement's room now."

"Clement's room?"

"Yes. He has a room here, doesn't he?"

"He had one. It's no longer his."

"Is it occupied?"

"Not presently."

"I'll still see it then."

Lucy sighed. She plainly thought he had lost his mind and she did not approve. She crossed to the window, closed the shutters, and strode into the corridor. "It's this way, sir."

He followed her to a corner room at the rear of the house. She stood back from the door after pushing it open. The shutters on the windows — there were two and on a sunny day this must have been a pleasant, well-lighted room

— were closed and it was as dark and gloomy as Muryet's chamber. But there was enough light to see that it had been stripped of all personal items. Even the mattress was gone from the bed.

"When did this happen?" Stephen asked.

"After Clement's arrest. The mistress had no need for him, since she did not inherit the business. She had William clean out the room."

Stephen nodded slightly. Clement had been Baynard's chief bailiff and had managed the draper's day-to-day business operations as well as having been deeply involved in Baynard's spying. Stephen had heard that Baynard's will left his business to a nephew, since he had no living children except for an illegitimate daughter, and that Olivia had received only a small income and a life estate in this house as her dower portion of the marriage property. He wondered to what extent the sumptuousness of the house concealed looming poverty. It was not surprising then that Olivia was discharging staff. "What became of Clement's things?"

"They were put in the loft in the stables. There is no need to go looking for them though," she said anticipating Stephen's question. "He has retrieved his goods since his release."

Chapter 7

Stephen returned to the hall. The two women were seated before the fire drinking warm cider with blankets thrown over their legs.

"Did you find what you sought?" Olivia asked.

"No," Stephen said.

"I'm so sorry," she said politely.

"Thank you, Mistress Baynard, Lady Margaret," he said with a bow, taking his leave. "If you learn anything about Makepeese, you will contact me?"

"Doubtless," Olivia said.

Stephen turned to go. He thought he heard Margaret hiss, "Olivia!"

Olivia coughed. "Sir Stephen, dinner will be served in a hour's time. Would you care to stay and keep two old widows —"

"Young widows!" Margaret said.

"Young widows," Olivia said, corrected. "Would you keep us company on such a dreary day? Surely that would be preferable than to chasing about in the wet."

Stephen thought of Christopher a prisoner at the castle and was about to say, no, I don't mind the wet. Then he remembered he had forgotten to inspect the study. He shouldn't rely on Valence's description, but should see it for himself. If he was going to do that now, he couldn't politely refuse. "I would be delighted."

"Good!" Olivia said. "Then Lucy will fetch you a chair and some hot cider — or would you prefer mulled wine? — and you can relax beside us."

There was an elaborate ivory chess set on a table whose top was inlaid with gray and white slate squares as the board. He challenged Olivia to a game, but she demurred. "Play Margaret instead," Olivia said. "She is the devil's own chess player. I've never known the man who could beat her."

Margaret scowled briefly, as if she had smelled something spoiled. But then she smiled brightly and accepted the challenge.

Stephen had thought that Olivia was exaggerating, but he found that Margaret was a formidable opponent. She played aggressively, quickly dominating the center and then mounted an attack on his left, where he had sheltered his king.

It didn't help Stephen's game that he found it hard to keep his eyes off her face and on the board. Once her foot brushed his calf. It did not instantly withdraw, but lingered there a moment. His first impulse was to jerk his leg away, for touching her in anyway was improper. But he froze. She did not seem offended at the contact. She looked up at him and smiled. He felt as though he could turn into a puddle on the chair. She withdrew the foot and moved a pawn.

Though Margaret played hard and well, she made a couple of oddly amateurish mistakes toward the end that allowed him to slip a bishop into checkmate.

"I'm afraid I've met my match. You play so well, sir," she said as they rose for dinner.

By this time, two dinner tables had been set up, a small one for Olivia, Margaret and Stephen, and a second larger one for the servants. Stephen had expected to see a bigger household, but Olivia's establishment was small. There was only Lucy and another two maids, two grooms and general handy men, a laundress, and an elderly gardener. Two other tough-looking men were present as well. Stephen learned they served Margaret. It seemed odd that she had servants who looked like soldiers, but she told him that they were old retainers of her father's and had come into her service when he died. "I couldn't turn them out," she said. "Their families have served ours for two hundred years."

Dinner, the main meal of the day which often dragged on for course after course at wealthy households, seemed to take no time at all. Stephen had little recollection of anything that was served except for little roasted hens in a mustard sauce and a delicious curry at the end.

He spent the entire time deep in conversation with Margaret. Olivia seemed to have lost her tongue and ate silently, staring at the fire. But Stephen had forgotten she was there. Margaret, for her part, was full of questions. She showed a great deal of interest in his experiences in Spain, and he found himself talking about the beauty of Spanish sunsets, the grandeur of Cordoba, the arid plains, the vast horse herds of central Spain, and things he would rather have forgotten, like the fearful chant of the Moorish cavalry just before the charge. He didn't tell her everything, though. There were things he held back: Taresa and Christopher. Along the way, she let slip bits of information about herself. She was twenty-one. She had a son, four. She was from an old family in Herefordshire to the south and west, well off but not fabulously wealthy.

At the close of the meal, after Lucy brought bowls of water and towels for washing their hands, Stephen asked to see Baynard's study. Olivia looked as though she'd rather be doing something else, but she led Stephen and Margaret upstairs to the front of the house.

The library was exactly as Stephen remembered it: A smallish eight-by-ten foot room with windows on two sides for light, a writing table with a large slanted writing box on top, and shelves holding a dozen books.

Margaret looked around the room and said, "So this is where Ancelin did his work."

"Some of it," Olivia said in a rather dark tone.

"Pleasant," Margaret said.

"If you like being cooped up with pens and parchments," Olivia said with the slightest hint of resentment.

Stephen crossed immediately to the table and the writing box. He tried the lid. It was unlocked and swung up to reveal parchments and vellum sheets and some expensive Italian paper stuffed inside as though whoever had looked at the materials last had stuck them hurriedly back in the box. Even though he had already seen everything here, he went through the documents slowly a page at a time, as if in the hope the list would be there and Valence had merely missed it. But of course it was not there. Most of the documents dealt with household issues, bills, lists of purchases, a long thick roll of accounts. It looked as though anything related to Baynard's spying had been removed.

He returned the documents and closed the lid. Then he knelt down and examined the hinges at the back. One of the pins was missing, as he expected it would be. He had got in the box without the key before by poking out the pins. He had time to return only one of them before Clement and Muryet had come to find out what he was doing in the study. The other pin was just as he had left it. One end showed the barely visible prick mark left by the point of his dagger, which he'd used to drive the pin back into place. It did not appear that whoever had stolen the list had got in the same way he had. They had used a key.

"How many keys are there to this box?" Stephen said, straightening up.

"Only one that I know of," Olivia said.

"Master Baynard kept it?"

"Yes, on a little chain around his neck."

"It would have been with him when he died, then."

"I would assume so. I've no reason to think otherwise."

Stephen tried to remember if he had seen such a chain on Baynard's body when he examined it. But he had not had Baynard stripped. He'd only pulled up the man's shirt to examine the death wound in his back.

"Who fetched the body?" he asked.

"Howard Makepeese and one of the grooms."

"Did they help prepare him for burial?" Whoever prepared Baynard would have removed his clothes and jewelry, washed him, redressed him, and sewn him in his burial shroud. They would have removed the chain.

"No. I did that."

It was the widow's duty, although in poor households neighbors or close relatives spared her the burden. Servants took the helpers' places in more wealthy establishments. For

Olivia to have taken on the duty implied she had really cared for Baynard. "The chain was with him then?"

"I think it was. I can't remember. I didn't remark it at the time." Olivia frowned. "Yes, I do believe so. It was. Yes, it was. You'll have to forgive me. I'm just a silly woman."

Stephen nodded. "It's hard to remember such little things. They don't seem important at the time. Where is the key now?"

"Why, with his personal effects, of course."

"Where are those kept?"

"In his room, naturally."

"They've not been disposed of?"

"Certainly not."

"Who has access to them? Could the servants —?" He let the question hang.

"I suppose they could. The room is not locked anymore."

He was finished here. He'd learned all the room had to reveal or that Olivia could tell him about the key. Anyone in the household could have taken it, anyone at all. He paused at the bookshelf and took down one of the books, the same one on sword-and-buckler fencing he had leafed through during his last visit and which he had particularly admired.

Margaret glanced at the work over his shoulder. "You are bookish too, along with your other accomplishments?" she asked playfully.

Stephen wasn't sure whether he should confess how he felt about books. Gentlewomen, especially the young, innocent and flirtatious kind like Margaret, were not known to be attracted to bookish men, and he desperately wanted to impress her, although the whole venture was such a lost cause. It was pleasant to flirt with her, but it couldn't possibly go any farther than that. He shrugged and said, "There was a large library in Cordoba. I went there a few times. There were enough books to make any man's head ache."

"I would like to see such a place. These dozen are the most I've ever seen in one spot." She turned to Olivia. "You've a fortune in books here."

"I had no idea," Olivia said, clearly surprised. She had shown no interest in the books, but she was interested now.

"You admire this one?" Margaret asked Stephen. The fencing book was beautifully illustrated.

"It's a work of art," Stephen admitted.

"It has a certain charm, I suppose, but it's not my taste."

"I wouldn't think so. There are several French romances there as well," he said, suddenly daring to tease her.

"Are there? Who'd have thought a man of business would care about them?" She took down a book and opened it. It was about gardening and herbs. "I rather fancy this one. I've manors to manage. This might be helpful. Olivia, could you part with it?"

"I — Yes, surely. Take it."

"Thank you, dear."

Stephen returned the fencing book to the shelf with some reluctance. The shelf proved to be a bit unstable, because the gentle force of the book's landing caused it to jar, which shook loose a leather cylinder hanging on a peg attached to the shelf. Stephen deftly caught the cylinder before it hit the floor. Heavily coated in wax, it was the kind of case used for transporting documents. The wax served to protect the contents of the case from the wet. He looped the strap over its peg, which stood next to another peg as if Baynard had hung a second such cylinder there. "I must be going," he said.

"Oh," Margaret said, disappointed. "If you must."

"I am a man of business myself," Stephen said. "And business calls."

"And what do you traffic in, sir?" she asked.

"Dead men and lost things," Stephen said.

The two women escorted Stephen to the door to say good bye, a courtesy he had not expected. In the ordinary run of things, Lucy should have shown him out.

"And where will you go now, Sir Stephen, in your search for lost things?" Margaret asked.

"I have an appointment at a bathhouse," he said.

But Margaret laughed. "I trust it is business and pleasure. We can all use a good rinse now and then. Good day to you, Sir Stephen. Shall we see you again? On business, of course."

Before he could answer, she shut the door.

Chapter 8

The moment the door to Baynard House closed behind Stephen, the worry returned, a coiled worm of anxiety mocking his ineffectiveness, whispering his hopelessness, sneering at Christopher's doom. Because if Christopher died, all that remained of Taresa except the ghost in Stephen's memory would die. Stephen pulled the hood of his cloak about his face against the drizzle and strode quickly down College Lane. He regretted that he had wasted so much time with the two women. They allowed him to pretend he had returned to his place among the gentry, and even to think that such a beauty as Margaret might find him interesting. But he had fallen too low ever to get back or to attract such a woman, and he could not afford the distraction.

He barely noticed the young urchin sitting on the stone fence outside St. Laurence's, idly twirling a stick in his fingers. The church had rung the hour of None some time ago, and school was letting out. Boys were streaming from the little stone school house on the north side of the church. Some of them shouted insults to the urchin as they passed through the gate. The urchin slipped off the wall and punched one of the speakers in the face, knocking him into a puddle on his fanny and producing a brown splash that dirtied the stockings of those nearby — a double insult in return, because no doubt the boys' mothers, like most mothers, had warned them not to get their stockings muddy. Before the other boys could pounce on the urchin, he had turned and dashed down the lane. The companions of the schoolboy who had been knocked down helped him to his feet. The schoolboy's mouth was bleeding, and Stephen heard indignant remarks and promises of revenge as he hurried by, hardly noticing, his mind fixed on what he had to do next. He had more important things to concern him than boys fighting.

At High Street, he paused at the corner for a herd of cattle that was being driven to the castle. The herd left the street churned to a nearly impassable pulp. Stephen had no choice but to cross it, and his feet sank to the ankles in the worst spots and made disgusting sucking noises when he pulled them free.

Going down Broad Street in bad weather always seemed more dangerous than going up. Ahead, in attempting to leap across the stream that was forming in the middle of the street, a prosperous looking glover lost his footing and fell headlong into the mud. Broad Stream had claimed another victim. The glover climbed to his feet, dripping and cursing. Stephen heard a child's high-pitched laugh behind him, but when he turned to see who made the noise, there was no one in sight.

Stephen managed to reach the gate at the foot of the hill without falling. Broad Stream flowing through the gate was almost ankle deep over the paving stones. Its sole benefit here was as a cleaner of boots, which only became soiled again when he passed out into the lower reaches of Broad Street on its run to the river bridge.

The Wobbly Kettle, a tall well-made timber building on the right opposite St. John's Hospital, was distinguishable by its sign, a red kettle tipped upon its side sloshing out a wave of blue water. Stephen went in. He wiped his feet on the mat and hung his wet cloak on one of the many pegs by the door.

The entry opened into a spacious hall that was well lighted because the owner had put glass in the windows. A serving girl thrust a clay cup of ale into his hand without being asked as she swept on her way to somewhere else. In contrast to the outdoors, it was hot and stuffy in the hall. There was only the central hearth in the middle of the floor for warmth but the fire going there was far higher than it needed to be. A few customers were playing backgammon and there was a table of card players bent over cheap cards painted on slats of wood.

The real business of the Kettle was in back, where there was an array of tubs, each secluded by embroidered curtains for privacy, and upstairs, where certain disreputable ladies plied their trade. Stephen strolled through the rear, trying to peek through breaks in the curtains without appearing to pry. He didn't see the person he was looking for. So he went back to the hall and started up the stairs. One of the girls paused on the way down and said, "Love, you're not supposed to go up there by yourself."

"I'm looking for Kate," Stephen said.

"She's with a client, love. It might be awhile, if you want her. Sure someone else won't do?"

"No, I'd rather see Kate."

The girl wrinkled her nose. It was hard to tell whether it was in disappointment or derision. She shrugged and continued down the stairs.

Stephen followed her and found a chair by the fire to wait. The heat was so intense from the blaze that he thought he might cook like meat on a spit. He pushed the chair back.

He could barely stand the wait at first and had several more ales than were good for him. He expected her to be not more than half an hour or so, but it was more than two before Kate appeared at last, and by then, Stephen was feeling pretty lightheaded, his sense of urgency blunted by drink and the seductive heat of the fire.

Kate caught him staring into the fire as she knelt at his elbow. "Hello, Steve," she said. Kate was not a great beauty, but she was pretty when she smiled. Her face was not ravaged by too much drink as some of the other girls. She was stick thin, except for ample breasts, which were practically in full view owing to her low-cut bodice. She had reddish hair and very pale skin.

"Hello, Kate."

"You look sad. What's the matter? Having a hard day?"

Stephen wanted to tell her about his troubles, but he was reluctant to unburden on her. He said, "I think I'm drunk. In fact, I'm sure of it."

Kate sniffed the contents of his cup. "No wonder. Ted's been plying you with the hard ale." She tugged at his arm. "Can you make it upstairs?"

Stephen heaved himself to his feet. He was relieved to find that he didn't sway too much. He hoped no one noticed. "I think so."

Kate paused at the bottom of the stairs to light a candle from the rack there. Then they went up to a room at the back. They needed the candle to see because it was dark and gloomy in the upper reaches of the house, shuttered up as it was against the storm.

Kate closed the door and set the candle in a holder on the wall. Stephen stood in the center of the room. There was nowhere to sit but on the bed, and since he had come for something else, the bed did not seem the right place. But Kate gently pushed him until the backs of his knees met the edge of the bed and he flopped down. She started to draw the string holding her bodice in place but Stephen held up a hand to stop her.

"I didn't come for that," he said.

"No?" Kate looked disappointed. "What did you come for?" She sat on his lap and took his head in her hands. She stroked his temples. He closed his eyes. He felt like purring when she did that. "Feel better?" she asked.

He nodded. His head fell to the crook of her neck. Like all the girls here, she used perfume. Some did so heavily, and you could smell them from ten feet away. Kate was more sparing. She smelled like a little flower. It was nice, he thought. Taresa used to sit on his lap like this. He imagined he was with her, not Kate. All the tension seemed to drain away. He ought to come here more often and get drunk and imagine things that couldn't be.

He took a deep breath and said, "I need some information, Kate." He could have asked anyone at the Kettle, including the owner, Ted, and got answers. But he trusted Kate most of all not to lie.

There was a slight catch in her breathing. "What do you need to know, love?" she asked into the top of his head.

"I need to find somebody."

"Who might that be?"

"A fellow named Howard Makepeese. Know him?"

He felt her nod. "Sure. He comes here. Came every Thursday with that man who had his neck broke."

"Muryet."

"That's the one. Thick as thieves, those two."

Stephen felt her chuckling. "What's so funny?"

"Well, Muryet was one of the odd boys, if you know what I mean."

"So I've heard."

"He was using Makepeese as cover. They'd come in together, acting as if they were after the girls. Makepeese would take one and Muryet . . ." She paused. "I shouldn't tell you the rest. It's a secret."

Stephen squeezed her waist gently. "I won't tell, I promise."

"Ted will be furious if he found out I told you."

"Cross my heart."

"Soldiers don't have hearts."

"I'm not a soldier any more. It grew back."

She drew back and looked into his eyes. He noticed for the first time that they were not fully green. There were little flecks of brown and blue in them. After some thought, she said, "There is a secret club. It meets here once a week, on Thursdays." She stroked his cheek with her fingers. "The members are odd boys. There would be about twenty of them if you got them all in the same room at once, though they don't all show on Thursdays. They come in, like this Muryet fellow, flirt with the girls down below and pretend to choose one of us. But when they get upstairs, the real choosing starts and they go off with each other. Or more often, they go to the baths together, where nobody asks any questions if two boys want to share a tub."

"And Ted knows about this?"

"Of course. How could he not know? Very little goes on here that Ted doesn't know about. He wouldn't be in business long if he was that blind."

"Twenty? As many as twenty?"

"Yeah, I think so." She laughed. "You've be surprised who some of them are. One's on the Twelve, another's a deputy bailiff, and yet another's on the council of the draper's guild. Some of them are even married."

"Good God." The Twelve were the town's aldermen, the main governing council. "What about the others?"

"A pretty mixed bag, some craftsmen, some laborers. A farmer or two from the country." She frowned, worried. "You're not thinking about doing something about this, are you?"

He sighed. He should do something, despite the promise. This kind of behavior was against the law. But it was impossible to stamp out and officialdom tended to look the other way as long as the odd boys kept their heads down and didn't draw attention to themselves. "No. It's none of my business."

She looked relieved.

"Did Muryet have a favorite?"

Kate concentrated. "Well, they all went round the circle often enough, but I think there was one he preferred more than anyone else."

Stephen waited, but she said nothing more. So he prompted her, "And his name is?"

"You really want to know?"

"I think I do."

"If I tell you, you'll go to him, and then it'll get out that I let slip."

"I'll be as discrete as a dove's wing. I have to know. Muryet wasn't killed by a fall. He was murdered. Somebody, for some reason, twisted his head all the way round, like you'd wring the neck of chicken. His favorite might be able to lead me to whoever did it."

Her mouth formed an O. "What a pleasant life you lead. Glad it isn't mine. I hate the dead." She shuddered. What she really meant was that she feared them, and through them death itself. She said, "All right, then. His name's Jonathon. He's a lay brother at St. Johns."

St. Johns Hospital — right across the street. Stephen couldn't help laughing. Simon, prior at St. Johns, had tried unsuccessfully to shut down the Kettle a few years ago because a few of the brothers had patronized it, violating their oaths of celibacy. The dispute had been settled when Ted had pledged not to let any of them in. "How does he manage it?"

"He comes in the back with the water boys and wood carriers. Pays Ted a little extra for his silence."

"That gets the job done. I wonder what excuse he gives old Simon to get away."

"You'll find out, I'm sure." She drilled a finger against his chest. "You have a way of worming things out of people that they don't want to tell."

"Worming things out? What about worming things in?"

She regarded him with narrowed eyes. "I thought you weren't in the mood."

"I wasn't, but I am now. You cheered me up."

"You dog."

"Always. Shall I howl for you?"

"No, you'll just frighten people."

Stephen swung Kate around on the bed and knelt between her legs. He pulled up her gown. She had no underwear on. Her patch was as red as her hair. He lowered himself onto her.

She pushed his shoulders up. "I want to look at you while you do it," she said. "I like to look at you."

He closed his eyes and yielded to the moment. But the face that floated before his inner vision was not Kate's, or even Taresa's. It was Margaret's.

"I thought you were looking for Howard Makepeese," Kate said as she climbed out of bed.

"I haven't forgotten. I was distracted."

"You're so easily distracted. Just like a man."

Stephen tied up his breaches. He hadn't noticed until now how cold it was in the room.

Kate held out her hand and beckoned with her fingers. Naturally, although they were something like friends, he wasn't going to get away free. Stephen dumped the contents of his purse into his palm. There were only three pennies there. Kate took two.

"Talk isn't cheap," she said.

"It never is, is it," Stephen said. His fingers closed around the remaining penny. It was all the money he had left. He was acutely aware how little separated him in reality from Harry's lot. He needed to do something about that, but he wasn't sure what.

Kate made her pennies disappear into a purse that hung on a cord between her breasts. "Being coroner doesn't pay much."

"Sir Geoff's slow with my wages." Geoffrey Randall was the king's appointed coroner, but he suffered from gout and old age, and he seldom stirred from his manor east of Ludlow to carry out his duties. He had hired deputies for that.

She patted him on the head. "Poor boy. That's why you don't come more often, isn't it."

"What about Makepeese?"

"Oh, him. Yes, well, he lives with his mother now. She has a house in Upper Galdeford. Lives right down the street from my mum." She put her nose to his. "Known that boy all my life. A useless dog. Tried to rut me even when I was married. Caught me in the orchard and wouldn't take no for an answer. Arnold ran him off." She looked momentarily wistful. Arnold had been her husband. He was dead now.

Stephen nodded and stood up. "Thanks."

As they moved together toward the door, Kate said, "Don't worry about Ted. I'll settle up with him about the ales."

"You're an angel, Kate."

"Of course I am. All the boys say so."

Chapter 9

It was twilight when Stephen pulled his hood up in anticipation of the rain as he stepped outside the Wobbly Kettle. But the rain had stopped, and the clouds overhead, crawling to the east, were shredded and broken, revealing a purple sky in which one or two stars winked feebly. To the west, beyond Whitcliffe, the sun had set. It was so cold now that Stephen could see his breath. The air smelled metallic from the rain but fresh and clean, despite the undercurrent of stale wool from the fulling mill beyond the bathhouse and the acrid, nose-wrinkling aroma of a tanner's that lay farther up the Teme.

Stephen paused before the imposing whitewashed stone bulk of the main building of St. John's Hospital. He debated going in, but it was nearly Compline and no doubt the brothers would be going to services if they weren't there already. The prior would not allow the disturbance. Events had bought that lay brother Jonathon a reprieve. He felt disgusted with himself. He had wasted the day.

It was almost two-hundred yards up Lower Broad Street to the gate, and by the time Stephen had waded there through the mud, the gate was barred. He pounded on it with his fist. "Gip, you old bastard! Open up."

There was a long pause before Gip, the warden at the gate, finally answered. "What should I do that for?"

"Because I want to get in."

"That's what everybody says, but I've got orders. Nobody goes in or out after sundown. Council's orders, they are. I never break my orders. Who is this anyway?"

"You know who it is, damn you — Stephen Attebrook, and I'm on crown business."

"Attebrook, you say. Crown business! You've been down to the Kettle. I saw you."

"No, you didn't. It was just somebody who looked like me. Now open up."

A small panel in the gate opened instead of gate itself, and Gip's frog-like face appeared in the aperture. "Was too you. I ain't that blind."

"Are you suggesting that a man of my position would lie?" Stephen asked archly with exaggerated offense.

"I ain't met the man yet who wouldn't lie when it suited him," Gip said. "Or at least seriously stretch the truth. No offense to you, your honor. Throwing your hard-earned cash away on drink and the lasses down there and you don't want folks to know. Yer secrets are safe with me, they are." Gip's hand appeared beside his face, palm up. "What you got for old Gip, tonight, governor? Or do you want to stand there till dawn in the wet, eh?" He chuckled.

No doubt Gip made a tidy living collecting from people like Stephen who were late leaving the Kettle and who needed to get back into town. Gatekeepers weren't supposed to let people in after sundown, but they often did for an off-the-table fee. Stephen dug out his last penny and pressed it into the waiting palm. Gip retracted his hand and closed the panel. There were a few bumps and thumps, then the gate swung open enough to admit a man on foot. Stephen stepped through the gap and Gip pulled the gate closed and struggled to drop the heavy bar.

"Thank you, Gip," Stephen said.

"Yer welcome, yer honor." Gip tugged his tattered wool cap and grinned. The light, unfortunately, was just good enough to see the single tooth he still retained, which hung crookedly beneath his nose. "Any time. And don't you worry about yer secrets. I'm good at keeping secrets, I am."

"I don't doubt that."

"Lots of secrets in this town that people don't want others to know. You'd be amazed, really amazed, at the things that folks do. In the daylight they act all proper like, but in the dark or behind closed doors — well, things are different, real different."

"So Harry tells me."

"Oh, he's a stout lad, that Harry, even if he's all deformed now. Knows how to keep secrets too, though he don't get the same profit from it as me."

"You're a good man, Gip. I know I can count on you."

"Oh, you can, you sure can."

"Tell me, Gip, did you see William Muryet and Howard Makepeese Thursday night?"

Gip's eyes got shifty. "I don't know as I did."

"Muryet's dead now, you know."

"Even the dead got secrets. You got to respect that."

"You want to know a secret about Muryet?"

Gip looked startled. "What?"

"He was murdered."

"I heard it was a fall. Fell down some stairs visiting a — a doxie."

"I know what he was, Gip, and he didn't run with the lasses."

"Oh, you heard about that."

"So did you see him and Howard Thursday?"

"Just so you know, there's nothing between him and Howard."

Stephen nodded impatiently. "I know. The question is, did you see them Thursday afternoon or evening?"

Gip nodded and spoke as if the words had to be pried from his tongue. "They came through the gate from the Kettle about this time of evening Thursday."

"Together?"

"Yeah." Gip hesitated, rubbing his hands on his smock as if locked in an internal debate whether to say anything more.

"What is it?" Stephen demanded.

"Well, they didn't give me a fee. Howard promised three times the usual for the both of them. Said they were about to make a killing and would be rich men, like by morning they'd be rolling in silver."

"What kind of killing?"

"They didn't say. Muryet hushed him up. Said they'd be back next day and pay me."

"Did Howard?"

"Did Howard what?"

"Come back and pay you."

"No, he didn't. I haven't seen him since, the bastard!" Gip was suddenly angry as if he had just remembered he had been cheated of his rightful graft.

Stephen nodded thoughtfully. "You've been a great help, Gip."

Gip's expression suggested he wasn't sure how or why, but he nodded in return. "Glad to be of service, yer honor."

Stephen trudged up Broad Street, going over in his mind all he had learned so far. Muryet had known a great deal about his dead master's secret business, of this much Stephen was convinced. As the de facto chamberlain, he would have had access to Baynard's effects, and could easily have secured the key to the writing box and stolen the list. He would clearly have known its value. So, he was certainly the thief. But for some reason, Muryet and Howard were partners and hoped to benefit equally from it. Yet as often happens, the two thieves must have fallen out over the proceeds. Perhaps Howard became greedy for the whole reward or they quarreled over the division. He was a strong man and could have killed Muryet. After the murder, he had fled. This made it all the more urgent that Stephen find Howard, but he realized that even then, he might not find the list. Howard could have, in fact probably had, sold it by now.

The dark mouth of Bell Lane loomed to his left, still as a crypt except for the patter of water dripping from the eaves. No one was about, even the watch, and behind every closed shutter Stephen imagined the inhabitants of the lane settling into bed. It was so dark, that he could barely make out his way; a half moon riding high to the south was obscured by clouds and provided no help.

A figure emerged from a gap between two houses. Stephen gave a start. Then he relaxed when he realized it was only a boy.

The boy stopped in front of him and held out his hand. He was the same boy Stephen had seen earlier in the day by St. Laurence church. "Sir," the boy said, "spare a farthing? I've had naught to eat since day before yesterday."

"I don't have a farthing." Stephen tried to go around him, but the boy dodged into his path.

"Surely, you do, sir. A man like you's got lots of pennies. Spare something for a poor boy like me, sir. A farthing isn't much, sir, to you, but to me it's a fortune."

"I said I can't help you," Stephen said, trying again to go around the boy, and again the boy dodged into his way.

"I'm starving, sir. Please!"

Stephen was not above helping the less fortunate when he could. But he had nothing to spare, so the boy's persistence was irritating. He tried once more to go round the boy.

Then the boy dodged once more into Stephen's way and grabbed his arm.

In the bigger towns, it was not unusual for a beggar to be so aggressive, even though it was not considered decent behavior. But in Ludlow, it was virtually unheard of. Anger rose like steam.

But only for a moment.

For Stephen heard feet behind him, and realized that he was in danger. This boy was no ordinary beggar. He had friends, violent friends.

Only that last moment's realization and a frantic effort to step aside saved him from a split skull. The blow meant for his head glanced off his right shoulder. The shock was intense. Stephen's arm felt as though it was paralyzed, and the wind was driven out of him. But if Stephen wanted to avoid another blow, he had to do something fast.

He grasped the boy by the collar with his left hand and threw him into the legs of the man who had just struck him. The assailant, club raised for another blow, was not prepared for this. He and the boy fell in a heap. Stephen kicked the man in the face. He flopped onto his back and didn't move.

For an instant, Stephen thought it was over. But it wasn't. There were two other men behind the one who had fallen. Ordinarily, the fact that Stephen had dropped one of his attackers should have been enough to deter the others. Predators want prey they can take easily without harm to themselves; not the ones who fight back. But these men must be desperate, for they came round the one on the ground on either side, while the boy scrambled to his feet and backed toward Broad Street, trying to drag the fallen man by the shoulders out of the way.

The better course was to run, but Stephen's bad foot left him a far slower sprinter than he had been and he wasn't confident he could reach the Broken Shield before the two caught him. Even if he did, he wasn't sure he could leap the fence and reach the safety of the yard in time.

Somehow finding the means, he drew his dagger with his right hand in the reverse grip and waited in middle guard. He backed slowly away, hoping that the sight of steel would deter the two where the knockout blow to their friend had not. But it didn't. They moved forward cautiously, but came on nonetheless.

The two exchanged a series of furtive glances as they spread apart. It was clear that they were experienced men, used to working together, and they knew the tricks a single victim could employ against them. They would not give him a chance to attack one of them, take him out, and attack the other. And they would not make the mistake of failing to attack Stephen together.

They were almost on opposite sides of him now, right and left, just out of reach, at a point where he could hardly keep both in view at once.

It was time.

No signal passed between them as far as Stephen could see, but they both sensed the moment, and they used it brilliantly. One struck high and one low, the blows coming from two sides so that if Stephen stood to parry one he would be felled by the other.

But Stephen did not stand still.

He slipped toward the man on his right, taking the blow on the dagger which lay along his forearm, hardly aware of the impact, and swept the club away. Without a pause, he stepped behind the man and, grasping him by the left shoulder, threw him to the ground.

There was no time or opportunity to do more to that. The man still on his feet was too dangerous. His blow to the legs had missed, but as an experienced man with a club, he had brought the stave in a circle to his left shoulder and prepared to launch a reverse blow from there without pause.

Stephen leaped forward, checked the man's arm at the elbow as he struck, and drove the dagger into his neck. The man's mouth opened in a soundless gasp and he sank to his knees.

Stephen put the dying man between him and the other, who was climbing to his feet.

It was now one to one, and the would-be robber didn't like the odds. He turned toward Broad Street and ran to where the boy was helping the robber Stephen had kicked in the face. The three of them jogged toward the corner and disappeared in the direction of High Street.

It was quiet again on Bell Lane, except for the patter of water from the eaves and the wet gurgles of a dying man, who fell silent with a few last soggy gulps and sagged backward, legs folded beneath him.

Breathing hard, Stephen glanced up and down Bell Lane. There was the faint glow of a lighted candle outlining the shutters of the widow who lived across the lane from the Shield, Mistress Bartelot. But that was the only indication of human activity. Round the corner on Narrow Lane a dog barked, and a cat hissed angrily. No shutters banged open, no one called out, no one stirred.

Stephen looked down at the dead man. It was a homicide, even if in self-defense, and there was always hell to pay under the law at a man's death, whatever the reason. The killer had to answer and buy a pardon, which Stephen could not afford to do.

"Shit," he said. He bent to wipe his blade on the man's coat. He dragged the body by the collar into the alley where the boy had waited to ambush him. He threw the man's club down beside him.

Then he walked on to the Broken Shield.

Chapter 10

The glassmaker's apprentice found the body the next morning. He ran straight to the Broken Shield for Stephen, who was sitting down to breakfast.

"Sir!" he cried, bursting with his news, "there's a dead man in the lane!"

The murmur of friendly talk that filled the hall died abruptly. Stephen put his hands in his lap so no one could see they were shaking slightly. He hoped his voice was composed, even bored. "A dead man? How inconvenient. Where?"

"In the alley beside my master's house." The boy, who was no more than eleven, panted like a race horse. He had not been the lucky fellow who had discovered the last dead man in the lane, a month ago with the murder of Ancelin Baynard. But he was the center of attention now.

"All right, then, I'll be there when I finish. Run along and make sure nobody disturbs anything."

"Right, sir." The child stood up straighter, bolstered by the importance of his mission, and raced out the door.

Gilbert, who like everyone else in the hall couldn't help hearing, hurried over. "Good heavens," he said, plopping onto the bench beside him, "that's two dead men in the lane in a month! Baynard and now this! We're going to get a reputation."

"Bad for business, eh?" Stephen said, still trying to keep his voice under control.

"Edith will say so. I'm sure she will. I just hope he wasn't a customer."

With some effort, Stephen forced himself to speak lightly. "Good God, if he was, people might say you've been serving poison."

"I'll thrash anyone who does," Gilbert said stoutly, although it was hard to imagine the round little man thrashing anybody. He saw that Stephen was in no hurry to rise to the occasion, so he rose himself. "Well, I'll summon the lads," he said, meaning the jury. "They ought to be here by the time you're done."

"Thank you, Gilbert."

Stephen ate slowly and carefully, conscious of the glances that were thrown his way by the guests in the hall. When the last of the bread and cheese was gone, he went out to face what he had done.

A crowd of perhaps two dozen people had gathered at the head of the alley. When Stephen and Gilbert pushed through them, he found the boy importantly posted with his arms out, making sure no one got too close. Stephen wouldn't have minded if they pawed over the dead man. As it was, he was glad to see their trampling about at the head of the alley had erased any sign that the dead man had been killed elsewhere and dragged to this spot.

"Thank you, Oliver," Stephen said to the boy. "You can go now."

Of course, the boy didn't go anywhere except to the front of the crowd so he could gawk with everyone else.

Stephen saw William Brandone and Thomas Tanner in the crowd, along with most of the other jurymen. "Anybody know this man?" he asked, gesturing toward the dead man, who lay on his back. He had been short and stocky in life with massive shoulders and thick brows. The top of his right ear was missing; it looked like an old wound.

There were shakes of the head throughout the crowd.

"No," William said. "He's a stranger."

"Well, you've seen what there is to see," Stephen said. "Might as well get started canvassing the neighbors. They might have seen or heard something."

After the jury had split up to question the neighbors, a task made easier because most of them were here already, Stephen made an elaborate show of examining the ground around the body. Then he had the dead man carried back to the inn. Gilbert ordered a table set up just inside the doorway of the stable, where there was light enough to see well, and the body was laid out on it.

A few curious stragglers lingered in the yard, hoping for more exciting views, and there were a few faces peering out of the windows of the inn.

"Get out of here! Shut those windows!" Stephen shouted at them. "What are you gawking at!"

"You're testy this morning," Gilbert said.

"It's that lumpy bed you've given me. I spent half the night awake."

"Probably a guilty conscience," Gilbert said.

Stephen's heart skipped a beat.

Gilbert went on, "We should see you in church more often. Confession is a tonic for lack of sleep."

"I'm not the confessing kind."

"It's your loss."

Gilbert bent to examine the wound on the neck. "A stabbing," he murmured. He took out his measuring stick and laid it alongside the wound, which was a little puncture in the man's neck only slightly crusted with blood. "Two inches wide. Let's see how deep it is." He produced the slat of wood they used to measure the depths of wounds and held it out to Stephen. "Would you like the honors?"

Stephen shook his head.

Gilbert sighed. "Leaving the dirty work to me, are you, as always?" He fed the slat into the wound. When it would go no farther, he paused to mark the depth and pulled it out. "Eleven inches at least," he said. "That was some knife. More like what a gentry man would carry than a common man."

"Yes," Stephen said.

"It's made a nasty wound. Through the neck and throat and down into the chest. It could even have reached all the way to the heart. No way to survive that." He shuddered as if thinking what it would be like to receive such a wound.

"Probably not."

"The body's stiff, too. And cold. What do you think it means?"

"He's been dead a while."

"Half a day, probably," Gilbert mused. "Don't you think?"

"I suppose so."

Gilbert paced in the doorway, thinking deeply. He paused for a moment, hand on the door handles, and seemed about to close them when Harry approached from across the yard where he had been working the crowd in the lane.

"Oh, hello, Harry," Gilbert said. He was not pleased at the interruption, but since the stable was Harry's home, he didn't seem inclined to deny him entry.

"You must be feeling better," Stephen said, glad to have something other than the dead man to talk about.

Harry grinned. Then he sneezed and blew his nose on a rag. "Can't resist a crowd, especially when it's right on the doorstep. Crowds are where money's to be made, lads. Can't let a little fever keep me from such easy profits." He settled against the wall, clearly intent on watching.

"Working on Sundays?" Stephen asked. "I'm surprised at you, Harry. It's supposed to be a day of rest."

"I take my work as I find it," Harry said. He nodded toward the body on the table. "Same as you."

Gilbert regarded Harry for a moment, then closed the door. He held out his hand. "May I see your dagger, Stephen?"

Feeling suddenly as if he had been struck naked, Stephen handed him the weapon.

Gilbert turned it over in and over, examining it closely. Then he held its hilt up to the wound. "Interesting," he said. "Very interesting."

"What is?" Stephen said flatly.

"The blade is the right width to have made this wound. And notice this bruise on one side of the wound. It matches the cross on your dagger exactly in length and width. Imagine that."

"Yes, imagine that."

Harry came away from the wall, intense interest on his face. "I thought dead men can't bruise."

"Oh, they can," Gilbert said. "They can. It's not unusual when a dagger is rammed stoutly home that its hilt leaves just such a bruise. I've seen this kind of mark often enough." He handed the dagger back. "At least you had the sense to wash off the blood. I thought you looked a little grim last night when you came in. I attributed it to your worry over Valence and your son. It seems you had something altogether different vexing you. Do you want to tell us what happened?"

There was no point in concealing anything. The three of them shared the knowledge of a secret death, which involved a body disposed of in the former latrine pit only fifty feet from where they stood. Stephen recounted the attack tersely, but spared no details.

When he was finished, he could practically hear the dust drifting in the shafts of sunlight that pierced the cracks in the stable's wooden walls.

"Well," Gilbert said, distressed.

Harry spat fiercely. "Had to've been Nigel FitzSimmons, the bastard. He's got no honor." Only last month, Stephen had been in a private feud with Nigel FitzSimmons, Earl Simon de Montfort's chief spy, provoked by Stephen's killing of FitzSimmon's cousin. The dead man in the latrine had been one of FitzSimmon's agents, sent to kill Stephen, but who had died instead. Ultimately, Stephen and FitzSimmons had fought a duel across the river in Ludford on Michaelmas and Stephen had won. That should have put an end to the affair if FitzSimmons was a man of honor.

"It would seem so," Gilbert said. "It's hard to believe ordinary robbers would have been so persistent."

"But what if it wasn't?" Stephen asked suddenly. Although FitzSimmons was an enemy, he didn't want to believe he had violated his oath to end the feud. Honor meant keeping your word and dealing fairly and honestly with people. It was the glue that held society together; without it there would be nothing but unchecked greed and chaos.

"What if what wasn't?" Harry asked.

"What if it wasn't FitzSimmons."

"It had to be him. Who else wants you dead? You can't trust those gentry bastards," Harry snorted. "All that honor stuff is crap. They speak it while they indulge in robbery and plunder and take whatever they want." He squinted at Stephen.

Stephen's mouth twitched. He could feel anger rising. "Your opinion doesn't count."

"Oh, course it doesn't. I'm just a farm boy with no legs. A person like that's not allowed an opinion."

"Enough!" Gilbert's voice cracked like a whip. This display of command was so unexpected and out of character that Stephen and Harry gaped at him. In silence that followed, Gilbert rubbed the bald dome of his head and said, "Do you want the whole inn to hear? Let's back up and deal with first things first. Stephen, you're sure no one saw or heard anything?"

"As far as I know."

"Then the jury should learn nothing. We can put this death down to homicide, assailant unknown. The jury won't need any coaxing to make such a finding, particularly since this fellow isn't a townsman. There's no one to care about him and make a fuss over his death. His bandit friends surely won't say anything. The next thing is, what do we do to keep you safe?"

"I'm safe enough."

"No, you're not. The next time you might not be lucky. And whoever it is, FitzSimmons or not, there is bound to be a next time. Since they failed once, they'll be sure not to fail again. All the care in the world is not proof against attack." Gilbert let out a deep breath. "You'll have to leave."

Chapter 11

"It's for your own good, really," Gilbert implored. "You must go."

Stephen shook his head. "Where? With what? I spent my last penny last night getting back in the town."

"Sir Geoff has been slow with our wages," Gilbert admitted. "But you've got three horses. You could sell one of them."

"No. I won't do that."

"Well, then, surely your cousin the earl will give you shelter now, when you explain the danger."

"Run to Eustace? His hospitality wasn't warm when I turned up before. He couldn't wait to get me out of his house and into this lowly position."

"Lowly!" Gilbert said, a bit stung.

"I could hardly get lower than this if I was shoveling manure."

"I had no idea you thought that way. Goodness, what you must think of the rest of us."

Stephen suddenly realized he had insulted Gilbert, which he hadn't intended. "Sorry. I didn't mean that."

"I think you did. I really think you did. Well."

"He's just bitter," said Harry. "He used to be rich and now he's poor and stumping around on a game leg, and he can't get used to it."

Gilbert looked thoughtfully at Harry. "Be careful what you say, Harry. You might inflame him even more."

"I said I was sorry." It felt odd to apologize to someone outside his own class. As a rule, the gentry never thought it had to justify itself or to make amends to commoners. But Stephen truly was sorry he had offended Gilbert.

"Apology accepted. Let's get back to business. The earl. Why not go to him?"

"You forget he gave my son to Valence. What good is he to me now?"

"But after this? Won't he change his mind? Your life's in danger. You son's life could be in danger. What if these killers strike at the boy if they can't get to you?"

Stephen was startled. He hadn't thought of that possibility. "You really think they might?"

"Men so vicious as to stab you in the back in the dark would not hesitate to strike down a child, if it suited their purposes." Growing excited, Gilbert forgot that none of the attackers had drawn a blade.

Stephen frowned. He said, "Valence won't give the boy up or let me go. He wants the list too much."

"Ah," Gilbert said. "There is that problem, isn't there."

"There is something I want to do, though. But I'll need your help. It will be a lot to ask of you."

Sunday's first mass of the day took place just after dawn at the hour of Prime. Edith, in deference to her husband's desire not to be roused so early on the week's day of rest, felt it proper that the couple attend the second mass, which occurred two hours later, at Terce. There was still time to make that ceremony, if they hurried, and Edith hustled Gilbert out into the street and there was nothing Stephen could do to save him. Stephen made the mistake of following a bit too closely, and Edith paused so he could catch up. She took him by the arm, as if he was a misbehaving son, and forced him to walk with them up Broad Street. But when the three reached High Street at the top of the hill, Stephen managed to break free. He left a peeved Edith standing there, hands on her hips. Then she linked her arm with Gilbert's and they crossed the street to St. Laurence's, merging with groups of town citizens flowing to the parish church. Terce was the most popular Sunday mass and the best attended.

Stephen continued up High Street to the castle. As usual, the gate was open and he went through, nodding to the guard, who was leaning against the wall just inside. Normally, the gate guard had at least a stool to keep him company, but owing to the fact that Valence was still in residence, Henle the castellan had banned stools since Valence thought they contributed to sloth. Stephen himself opposed sloth in soldiers because it meant they were lazy, and lazy soldiers were on the road to defeat, but Valence carried his enmity to extremes. Stephen was glad to see that Valence was still here. His plan would be far harder to implement, if not impossible, had Valence gone back to his chief manor, which lay more than ten miles outside town.

But to be sure, Stephen said to the guard, "I'll bet you'll be glad when his worship is gone."

The guard spat and smirked. They knew each other from mornings together in the practice yard. "The bastard's taken over. Henle's about ready to pull his hair out. He can't tell anyone what to do without his worship interfering."

"It makes you wish you were out collecting taxes, doesn't it."

"I'd rather be doing anything than standing here."

Stephen crossed the vast outer bailey, which was deserted. Although the sky had cleared and the rain had stopped, the horse herd in the huge paddock to the left looked bedraggled, like beggars waiting at a palace gate for alms. The aroma of wet horse, manure, and mud hung in the quiet air. To the right, where the castle vegetable garden lay against the north and east walls, a pair of pigs were pulling at a slat in the garden fence. The pigs looked at him like a pair of conspirators who had been caught at their mischief. But when he did not reprimand them, they turned back to their work of trying to break through the fence.

Passing through the narrow gate into the inner bailey always seemed like entering another world. Everything was clean and neat, the timbers of the hall freshly painted black and the plastered squares between them as white as a nun's linen. Things always seemed to glow here with understated prosperity and wealth. This was where Henle lived, and like most lords he valued his comfort.

The inner bailey was small and gave off a compressed feeling, as if everything was squeezed together. The huge circular bulk of the inner chapel to the right, which took up much of the little space there was, compounded the feeling. It loomed there so out of place that it often seemed to Stephen that the castle had been built around it, although he knew the castle had come first.

A few people were loitering at the doors, servants mostly who were undoubtedly there because Valence expected everyone to attend the Terce mass. Most were watching a pair of boys who were wrestling and not doing a very good job of it, straining and grunting without a decision either way. Since everyone wrestled, everyone felt competent to shout instructions to their own favorite, and this made a racket. Stephen wouldn't have minded watching too, but he had other more urgent business. One of Valence's grooms, whom Stephen recognized, emerged and scolded the crowd for the noise they were making, then spoiled the game by running the boys off with a kick and a few choice words.

Stephen edged through the doors and stood at the back of the chapel. He surveyed the crowd, trying to spot Christopher's nurse, Gunnora. She was a short plump woman, and he could not find her in the press.

The chaplain was chanting something in Latin out of sight behind the hedge of bodies. He spoke good Latin and didn't mispronounce any of the words, a common failing of country priests who were often badly educated. But Henle could afford a chaplain who'd been to Oxford. The sonorous Latin words, which sounded like singing even when it was not meant to be singing, rolled through the air with the inexorability that only Latin possessed. Stephen smiled. You could announce you were on your way to the privy in Latin and it would still sound majestic. With some effort he could have made out what the priest was saying. Unlike most people here, Stephen had studied Latin, but more the reading than speaking kind. And he didn't care to make the effort. He had only been mildly religious, and since Taresa had died he had completely lost his faith. When she had fallen sick, he had clumsily tried to nurse her and when she had collapsed into her last sleep and it was obvious she would not awaken without a miracle, he had prayed and pleaded with God to save her. He had promised everything he possessed, including his own life. But she had died anyway. He could not forgive God for stealing her.

A hand touched his arm. This was not some casual brush in the crowd because the hand did not let go. He turned to see who it was and found himself looking down into the cool face of Margaret de Thottenham.

At any other time, he would have enjoyed meeting her. But not now.

"Good day, Lady Margaret," Stephen murmured, trying not to let his interest show.

She smiled at him. "I'm so glad to see you. We were wondering how your search was going. Olivia is desperate to know who killed Muryet."

"I'm afraid I haven't learned anything useful."

Her face fell. "Oh." Then she brightened. "But what is your next step? You must have a next step. What will you do now?"

Stephen sighed. The last thing he wanted was someone prodding him about what he was going to do next, even if it was a beautiful woman. Had it been anyone else he would have made some excuse and moved away. But his mouth said for him, "For what it's worth, I've learned that Makepeese went to live with his mother in Upper Galdeford." Not until he'd spoken the words did it hit him how thin and useless that information seemed.

"And you've been there to speak with him?"

"No, not yet."

"Why not? The trail will get cold if you don't act quickly."

Perhaps so. But there was something he had to do before he continued the hunt. He said lamely, "One's soul comes first, my lady. There is time yet."

She frowned. But anything she might have said was interrupted when Olivia came up as the crowd began filing through the main door. Olivia was flushed with excitement. Why should she would be excited over a mass puzzled Stephen, until it became clear that it wasn't the mass but an invitation to dinner by the Henles that had stimulated her. Townsfolk weren't casually invited to dine with the castellan's family, so this was a rare honor.

The two women chatted about the forthcoming social event while Stephen scanned the crowd. He spotted the nurse as she neared the door and moved to intercept her.

"Good day, Gunnora," Stephen said.

Gunnora looked nervous at being confronted by him, and made a shallow reverence in reply. "G'day, your honor."

Christopher was in her arms. At the sight of his father, he leaned forward and held out his arms. "Da!" he cried.

Stephen took the boy before he fell on the ground. It felt good to hold him. It had only been just over a month since they were parted, but already the boy seemed different: bigger and changed. He was already talking more English, which mixed oddly in with the Spanish that he already knew. At least Christopher was well fed and seemed happy. But Stephen couldn't hold the boy for long. It wasn't done to show public affection for one's children. He passed the child back to his nurse. Christopher squirmed in her arms and tried to get down, but Gunnora held him firmly.

"What happened, Gunnora?" he asked. "Why did Eustace give up Christopher?"

"I don't know!" she said.

"How could you not know? Lords have no secrets from their servants."

Gunnora dropped her eyes to the ground. "No one knows what they said to each other."

Stephen looked disgusted.

"My lord did not want to give him up," she said defensively, "but Valence insisted." She stepped closer and said in a lower voice, "There is something between them.

Valence has some hold over him. I don't know what it is, but it's powerful. They went into his lordship's chamber and when they came out it was done. Whatever it was, it frightened his lordship. I know it did. He tried not to show it, but I know it worried him. He made me go. To protect Chris and keep him safe."

Stephen nodded as if he sympathized and understood, although he was completely mystified. They walked out of the chapel into the bailey. "Will you be staying here long?"

"We're leaving tomorrow morning. Going to Haverford, it's said."

Stephen had heard of it, or course, although he had never been there. It was Valence's chief manor. "Valence is treating you well? They've given you decent rooms while you're here?"

"A small one, but quite comfortable."

As casually and as disinterestedly as he could, he said, "Which one is it? Those rooms above the hall can be so small and cramped and drafty. If you're not fully satisfied, I'll speak to Henle myself."

"There's no need, sir. It's the one on the third story at the back by the watchtower."

"There?" He pointed to the right toward a large square tower that loomed over the hall.

"Yes, sir," Gunnora said.

Stephen nodded. "That's a good room."

"You know of it, sir?"

"Yes. Smallish, but comfortable. The window lets in the morning light."

"That's the one, sir." She hefted the boy on her hip. "Now, if you don't mind, sir, we're off to the nursery."

"There you go," Stephen said. He wished he could follow them and watch Chris play. He had enjoyed sitting in the bailey of Rodrigo's castle in Spain and watching the boy play in the dirt alongside the other castle children. Taresa had abhorred allowing him to play in the dirt because he liked to eat rocks. The memory saddened him. All those other children were probably dead now, or enslaved. He doubted that many of Chris' playmates had survived the final assault on the castle.

He found Margaret and Olivia had not yet gone to the hall, where most of the other church-goers were headed. They were watching him and it would have been rude just to walk away without saying anything. So he approached, intending to find some excuse to get back to business as quickly as he could.

Margaret said, "You are a man of many parts. Soldier, king's officer, and evidently a student of the law."

"You've been talking to James de Kerseye." De Kerseye was a lawyer now and had once been something of a friend.

"He told us that the two of you once clerked for Lord Ademar at Temple Bar in London, but that you had a falling out with him."

"It was a long time ago," Stephen said, not wanting to talk about it.

"He also told us that Lord Ademar holds your son for your good behavior. Was that him?" She sounded genuinely concerned.

Stephen was surprised that de Kerseye would know that, and her concerned touched him. He nodded. "Yes."

"A handsome child. Will Lord Ademar harm him if you are not compliant?"

Stephen again was surprised: it was not obvious that Christopher was in danger. How could Margaret have foreseen that? He said, "I don't know."

"Death is often the fate of hostages," she said with unexpected grimness. "Then you mustn't lose a moment. You must find the list. What will you do now?"

Stephen said, "I'll have to go to Makepeese's house and see if he's there."

Margaret drew herself up and it was only then that Stephen realized how short she was — barely reaching his chin. "Then that's where we will go. Let's be gone. There's not a moment to lose."

Chapter 12

Stephen had not missed Margaret's "we" and not "you," and was turning it over in his mind, wondering what to say, as they walked together toward the narrow gate to the outer bailey. As drunk as she made him feel and as reluctant as he was to put aside the wine cup of desire, she would just be in the way. He had more important things to do today than find Makepeese and the thief of the list.

Then Olivia called out petulantly, "Margaret!"

Margaret stopped abruptly and swung back. "What is it, dear?"

Olivia looked stricken. "The dinner! We're going to miss it."

"Then you go."

Olivia leaned close so that only they could hear. "But I'm not invited. You're the one who got the invitation, not me. I'm only to be your guest."

"And you still will be. The steward knows that you came as my friend. He'll seat you even without me. You just go in as if you belong there. If anyone asks about me, tell them I've taken ill and have had to return to the house for a nostrum. Sir Stephen has agreed to escort me." She said in a more meaningful tone. "The ladies will understand that." Margaret pulled back and said more matter of factly, "This is your chance. Play it right and they will accept you, and then who knows what the future will hold."

"I can't do this by myself."

"Yes, you can. They know who you are and where you came from. Now that you are husbandless and without his baggage, you'll be more agreeable to them. You were brought up for this very opportunity. Now be strong. You know what to do."

Olivia stood there for a moment, quivering almost imperceptibly with anxiety and breathing hard. Her eyes darted from Stephen to Margaret and back again. "All right then," she said with sudden fierceness. She turned about and strode determinedly to the hall.

Margaret observed the effect of her words with a small satisfied smile. Then she said abruptly to Stephen, "Shall we go, sir?"

"If we must," Stephen sighed. For such force of personality to emanate from such a small person was unexpected.

They passed through the inner gate to the outer bailey. Stephen unconsciously increased his pace, as he often did when he was in a hurry. Margaret lifted her shirts and hurried to keep up. Unlike Gilbert, she did not complain about it. Stephen slowed for her when he realized he was walking so swiftly. He said, "This may not be a place for a lady."

"What do you mean? That Makepeese lives in a hovel? You think I'm not accustomed to hovels or to the poor? There are poor enough on my manors and I deal with them like anyone else."

"Well, it's not your affair, so there's no reason to . . ."

She did not let him finish. "I shall not stand by and see a good man's child put at risk if there is something I can do to help." Then she took his arm and said softly, "If there are women involved, and I am sure there are, I may be able to speak to them more frankly and persuasively than a man might do."

And that was that. He might as well try resisting a river.

She also had a way of getting him to talk about himself, which he normally did not do with anyone. Before they had reached the main gate she had pried out of him the facts of his indenture to Valence, a subject which he had never shared with anyone, as if his mouth was a clockwork and all she had had to do was turn a key to unwind him. "I was a little wild as a boy, always getting into trouble. My father thought I needed discipline. He was right about that, but he picked the wrong master. Eventually, I rebelled and ran away."

"And he lost his surety," Margaret said. Apprentices, especially those in professions such as the law, had sponsors who stood surety that they would complete the terms of their contracts. If they failed, the sponsor stood to lose the surety, which usually was a considerable sum of money.

"Yes. I disobeyed him and cost him money."

She laughed. "So, failing at law, you turned to soldiering? An odd switch."

"I always wanted to be a soldier, earn a fortune and retire to my manor." He shrugged. "It seemed like the only way to get one. My older brother was the favored one, you see. I got nothing."

"It does not seem you earned a fortune," she said delicately.

"I did, but I lost it." He sighed, thinking of the fortune he and Taresa had to leave behind when they ran for their lives — or rather, when she had carried him off, delirious with fever from his wound, just before Rodrigo's castle fell to the Moors. He tried to push the memory aside but it was too bitter and heavy. "All of it."

"Fortunes can be made again."

"Maybe."

She continued to pull out of him the most intimate things as they walked along High Street. He even spoke about his present work, which he did only because he had to to survive, and he even mentioned Taresa, although he skipped lightly over her, trying to conceal his sense of loss, which would not leave him, for no one wants to be burdened with someone's grief.

At the top of Broad Street, they met Gilbert and Edith, who were returning late from mass, probably because Edith liked to stop and chat with people at the church door. Gilbert blinked at the sight of Stephen and who was at his side. Stephen did not have a reputation in Ludlow for strolling about with beautiful women; even if he'd wanted such a reputation it would have been hard to earn because there just weren't that many available beautiful women here. After Stephen had made introductions, Gilbert asked a bit too anxiously, "All preparations are ready for tonight, though?"

"Tonight?" Margaret asked. "What's happening tonight?"

"Gilbert's taking a journey," Stephen said quickly in an effort to head off any further questions.

"Yes," said Edith with narrowed eyes and a suspicious tone. She didn't know the reason yet for the journey, either, and that bothered her. Stephen knew he would have to tell her this afternoon, and hoped that she would keep her objections to a minimum.

"Ah," Margaret said, making conversation, "where will you be going?"

"Oh," Gilbert said, "a short way into Shropshire. Not far."

"Is that it?" Edith said.

"Yes, my dear," Gilbert said, rubbing his round stomach. "It's business, as I told you. I shall not be long."

"It seems odd," Margaret said, "to start a journey of any distance in the evening."

"He means before dawn," Stephen said. "He's getting an early start."

"That's not what I heard," Edith said.

"You must have misheard me," Gilbert said.

"I distinctly did not mishear you," Edith said.

"Well, I meant to say before dawn. I really did." Realizing that too much had been said before someone not entitled even to have a hint of the secret, Gilbert said good day, and guided Edith away down Broad Street, who was put off to know a secret was afoot and to be deprived of further conversation with a new acquaintance.

"That was odd," Margaret said after they were out of earshot.

"Was it?" Stephen said as if he was disinterested.

"Doesn't he serve you?"

"Occasionally."

"I thought he is your clerk."

"When the occasion demands. Otherwise, his life is his own."

"I see," she said.

Across Broad Street, they entered the defile of Draper's Row, where the street narrowed considerably. Some of the richest men in town lived and not far along stood Ancelin Baynard's principal shop. The ground was churned up from the recent rains and the passage of cattle and other traffic. They clung to the margins, hugging the sides of the buildings to avoid getting caught in the mire. Some of the householders had put down planks, temporary expedients to prevent the hapless traveler from sinking into the muck, but balancing on them was a bit precarious. Stephen dared to take Margaret's hand to help her. Her fingers where soft, long and warm in the autumn chill. He was thrilled when she did not draw away but tightened her clasp with an eagerness that he risked fancying was more than casual politeness or a desire to avoid drowning. Was there hope? Or was he simply mad? He decided he must be mad.

Draper's Row wended for fifty or sixty yards, then opened into the expanse of Beast's Market, the confluence of four streets. The empty timber frames of vendors' market stalls stood to one side. Now that Margaret did not need the pretense of his assistance, she withdrew her hand and tucked both demurely into her sleeves. But she smiled and they made polite conversation as they waded across the market and passed through Galdeford Gate.

Just beyond the gate there was a food shop that sold little pastries through the window to anyone who happened by. Although it was Sunday, and nobody was supposed to be doing any business, the shutters were down, a woman sat in the window bundled against the chill, and the warm scent of fresh sweetbuns assaulted the nose. If she had been within the walls, the wardens would have had a sharp word with her, but since this was outside they had no authority and she had only the lord's bailiff and parish priest to contend with, both of whom were probably paid to look the other way. Margaret glanced at Stephen expectantly. He had no money and looked embarrassed. She dug into her purse and handed him a quarter-penny. "That should be enough for two," she said.

Stephen went to the window, bought two buns as instructed. He held out both but she accepted only one.

"I forgot until now how hungry I am!" Margaret said. She licked her fingers, which were drenched with honey from the bun.

Stephen watched fascinated at the way she pursed her lips. He had the sudden urge to kiss her right there in the street. He forced himself to look way. He really was going mad. He said, "Thank you."

"Which way now?" she asked.

Stephen pointed to the left where the road forked. "Up Upper Galdeford Street," he said.

"Let's not tarry then. I say, sir, are you going to eat that bun or wear it on your head?"

"I look silly enough as it is without a bun on my head," Stephen said, finally taking a bite. He started down Upper Galdeford Street.

"That was good," Margaret said, keeping pace. "I hope they have more left when we return."

"It's even more delicious because it's Sunday and forbidden," Stephen said.

Her elbow brushed his, an accident? "The forbidden is always more delicious, isn't it?"

"Sometimes it is."

Stephen only had to ask twice for directions to the Makepeese house and they were there in short order. The house was on the right some distance up the road toward Lowbridge. It sat just beyond a small ruined stone chapel surrounded by a wattle fence which cut a corner out of a broad meadow. The house's timbers and the plaster-covered wattle that filled the spaces between them were mossy and gray with age, but it had been thatched during the late summer and its roof still retained that brown color which was so attractive and easy on the eye. The house sat back from the road behind a thick oak, bare of leaves now, but which in summer must provide pleasant shade in the front yard. Normally, the ground around an oak was littered with acorns, but not a single one lay here, as if the ground had swallowed them up. Two planks bridged the shallow ditch along the road. Stephen crossed them and held the gate open for Margaret. A goat looked up from grazing on a sprig of grass and eyed the open gate as though contemplating a bid for freedom. Stephen closed and latched the gate with its loop of rope to prevent the dash.

A barefoot girl of about ten suddenly burst out of the house, glancing at them warily, grasped the goat by the ear, and towed it inside.

Stephen followed her to the door. An overturned flowerpot lay on its side to the left, smashed and spilling its soil and occupant, a spray of primrose which looked healthy and green. Someone had paid close attention to that primrose. A circular watermark on the bench by the door told Stephen where it had sat. It was odd that it had been knocked off and just left to lie there, for the house and yard were carefully tended, just like the plant: obviously poor but kept up.

The door was open and Stephen stood on the threshold, which was just a worn plank of wood that separated the dirt of the yard from the dirt of the floor inside. With the windows all shuttered, it was dim inside but he could make out the details. Directly to the right ran a wall pierced by a door which had to lead to the bier, holding goats from the smell. The living space opened to the left. A hearth smoldered in the middle of the floor, a black iron kettle dangling over it from a tripod. Beside the hearth were the house's main furniture, a rickety trestle table and two benches. A bed, or more accurately a straw-filled sleeping pallet, lay on the ground on the far side of the fire beneath a shuttered window. Ordinarily during the day such pallets were rolled up and put in the loft, which hung over the far left end of the room, and from which four children furtively gaped at the visitors. But this bed was occupied, although Stephen could not see by whom, for his view was blocked by a crone of a woman sitting on a small stool by the bed. The girl who had secured the goat emerged from the bier, raced across the room, and clambered up the ladder to the loft to join the other children.

The crone, whose brown cloak draped a bent and skinny figure, rose to face them. White hair writhed in disarray from beneath her linen cap. "Who are you?" she demanded in an unfriendly tone. "What do you want?"

"My name is Stephen Attebrook, and I'm looking for Howard Makepeese. I'm told he lives here now."

"He's not here," the crone said. "Don't bother looking around for him either. And don't you dare touch her or one of the children, or I'll have the law on you, quick as lightning. I'm not afraid to call them." There was a long pause. "Like some."

"I am the law," Stephen said, although from the look on the crone's face she either was not impressed or didn't believe him. "Why would I want to touch one of the children?"

"Huh," grunted the crone. She stepped to the fire and ladled some thick brown fluid from the kettle to a clay cup. She turned and knelt by the figure in the bed. Stephen caught a whiff of sulfur. "Here, dearie, try drinking a bit of this again. Let's go now."

Stephen edged to the side and saw that a woman occupied the bed. Someone had beaten her terribly. There were cuts about her eyes and mouth and her forehead and cheeks were splotchy with fresh bruises. When she opened her mouth to drink, he could see that her upper and lower front teeth were missing, the gums scabbed with blood — more fresh wounds. Yet despite her ravaged face, Stephen could see Howard Makepeese's handsome one in it, as if this was the feminine mold from which it had been cast.

"Is that Howard's mother?" he asked.

"Go away," the crone snarled over her shoulder.

"What happened here?" he persisted.

"None of your business," the crone said. "None of anybody's business."

The injured woman, who had been about to drink that thick stinking fluid, looked frightened at his questions. She shut her mouth and rolled painfully to face the wall.

"Damn it, man," the crone raged, "look what you've done! Don't interfere!"

"Stephen!" Margaret said. "Look here." She was standing by the open door to the bier. "You must see this."

Stephen crossed the room and leaned around the door jam. The room held about a dozen dead goats. But all of them had their throats cut. The lone survivor — the goat rescued in the yard by the girl — chewed on some straw among the corpses.

Stephen swung around. "Who did this?"

"The devil did it," the crone said. "That's all you need to know." She waved him away and tried to coax the injured woman to the cup. "Now be gone, or I'll throw on a curse you. And I know how to make them stick, too, make no mistake."

"Someone came asking after Howard, didn't they," Stephen said.

The crone ignored him.

"Someone came and she would not tell. She would not tell and they killed the goats. First one, and when she still would not tell, another and another, until they were all dead, except the one, which they must have missed. When they did not have what they came for, they beat her. Isn't that the truth?"

"I'll not say a word," the crone said. "I wasn't here."

"And now you think I might beat the children until she talks, don't you."

The crone straightened up, having been successful at last in forcing her tonic into Mistress Makepeese. "The thought had crossed my mind, young man." She gestured at the children in the loft. "Their's too."

Stephen's eyes had adjusted enough to the dimness for him to see that they were terrified of him. "I'll not touch them. But I must find Makepeese. It's urgent."

The crone sat down on her stool. "Why? Nobody's ever thought much of him in the past. Just a rake and a wastrel, that boy. Good for nothing." The woman on the cot groaned and raised a hand. "Hush, Beth, you know it's true. Don't try to defend him any more. Look what it's got you. Years of fret and worry. All your beasts dead, your body wracked and ruined."

Mistress Makepeese tried to speak, but the noises she made did not form words that any of them could understand.

But perhaps the crone understood them. She said, "She won't talk because if she does Howard will die. He's her first born, you understand, and a charmer. The fool. She'd rather die herself than give him up."

While Stephen and the crone had talked, Margaret climbed the ladder so that her face was even with the floor of the loft. The younger children shrank from her, but the ten-year-old girl held her ground. Margaret implored, "We must find him. We mean no harm to anyone and will not touch you, regardless what you say. But if you keep silent the lives of many men and women, good men and women, may be forfeit. Your silence could condemn them. Please help us."

The girl spoke. "This isn't about the dead man in town?"

"No, not at all. It's something different entirely. Something much bigger than one man's murder."

"He didn't do it. They were friends."

"We don't think he did, but we think he knows who was responsible."

"You won't hurt him?"

"No," Margaret said, "I promise."

"We don't know where he's gone. They wouldn't tell us." They — Howard and his mother.

"Oh," Margaret said, disappointed. The trail had struck a dead end.

Suddenly, the girl lunged forward and kissed Margaret on the cheek. Margaret gave a start, but she did not draw back. The girl lingered close for a moment, then withdrew.

Stephen could see they were going to get nothing useful from any of these people. But he asked anyway more out of frustration than anything else, "Who did this? Who did this to you and your mother?"

The girl peeked at him over the lip of the loft. The struggle whether to answer him played across her face. She spat full of an adult hate, "Clement! Clement did it!"

In a daze, Stephen did not remember leaving the house or crossing the yard. The world did not seem to swim into view until he was some distance down the road toward town.

"It seems Valence has set two seekers after the list," Margaret said.

"No," Stephen said, sucking thoughtfully on his front teeth. "Clement is doing this on his own. He broke Mistress Makepeese's face only after he was sure she wouldn't tell him what he wanted to know. He did it so she wouldn't be able to tell me if she had a change of heart. He must think that if he recovers the list, he improves his chances of escaping the hangman. He also discredits me." He told her briefly how he had discovered Clement's complicity in the death of a certain Patrick Carter, an Irishman, and how that led to Clement's imprisonment on a murder charge. "He holds a grudge, you see."

"What will you do now?" Margaret asked.

"I don't know. Muryet had a secret lover. Perhaps he knows something."

"He did? Who is it?"

Stephen shook his head. "I promised not to reveal his identity."

"Surely you owe such a person no pledge of secrecy."

"I didn't make the pledge to him."

"To whom then?"

"I'm not free to disclose that either."

Margaret pouted, but the expression was more playful than serious. "Well, then, before you continue the hunt, you should at least have some refreshment. Let's stop in at Olivia's house. I'm sure that the cook will have something prepared."

It was past noon by the time they reached the house on College Lane. They let themselves in and emerged into the hall, which was empty. Their footfalls echoed in its vastness. No voices sounded anywhere in the house and no one came to see who had arrived.

The emptiness of the house did not seem to bother Margaret, although she must be used to servants rushing to attend her. She removed her calfskin gloves and laid them on the arm of one of the chairs before the fire. She turned to face Stephen. She said, "It seems Olivia has not come back. Dinner must have been a success for her. I'm so glad."

"You've known her a long time?"

"Since we were children. Our father's houses were near Adforton, less than a mile apart. We were together constantly. We had a secret place in the forest where we used to meet, an old forester's hut."

Stephen nodded, trying to think of something clever by which to take his leave. But nothing came into his mind, which was frozen by erupting desire. Here he was alone with her in this vast house, well, as much alone as anyone could be in such a place, because there had to be servants lurking somewhere.

Margaret took a step toward him. Her blue porcelain eyes were suddenly misty. Her lips parted with an odd uncertainty, a strange hesitation. She said almost in a whisper, "Stephen, if you want to kiss me, there's no one to see."

He crossed the narrow interval between them with quick, decisive strides. He put his hands on her thin waist and bent his face to hers. With a tremulous exhalation that was almost a gasp, she raised her face to his.

Their lips touched.

A long time afterward, Stephen sat up in bed. The shutters were closed against the chill of late October, and the room was dark, lighted by only a single candle on a table across the room. Feeble light leaked in around the edges of the shutters. It must be late, very late. Perhaps, he thought with alarm, too late.

Margaret rose to an elbow and touched his arm. The woolen blanket and linen sheet fell away to reveal her breasts and shoulders, white as ivory, smooth and perfect and miraculous. "Don't go yet. Please."

"I'm sorry. I have to. There's something I have to do. Something urgent. I can't put it off."

"What is it?" She stroked his hair and kissed his shoulder.

"Family business," he said.

"Family always comes first, doesn't it," she murmured and lay back on the pillow.

"I'm afraid so."

But as he rose, she grasped his arm and pulled him down. He thought she only wanted a kiss, which he gave her, long lasting and passionate. When they broke, her lips remained close to his.

Margaret said softly, "The girl told me something before we left."

"What?" Stephen said, surprised. He thought he had heard everything Howard's younger sister had said. "When?"

"When she kissed me."

"What was it?"

"Lucy knows. She said Lucy knows."

Chapter 13

Lucy was not at Baynard House and none of the other servants knew where she had gone. So there was nothing more that Stephen could do but attend to his other, truly urgent business.

When Stephen emerged onto College Lane, he saw from the angle of the sun and the long shadows that there was less than an hour till sundown — barely enough time to do what needed to be done. How could he have let himself be so distracted? He felt foolish and weak, but not so much that it drowned his exhilaration.

Gilbert, Edith, and Harry were waiting at the stables to the Broken Shield with the horses when Stephen hurried in the yard.

"Good lord, man," Gilbert said, "what have you been up to? Do you not know the hour?"

"I'm sorry," Stephen said. "I was detained."

Harry looked at him closely. "Detained at what?"

"None of your business."

Harry cackled, then sneezed violently. "Bet it wasn't business that detained you!"

Stephen could feel himself getting red despite the fact that there was no way Harry could know what he had been up to. "Back to your nest, you gutter rat, before you infect the rest of us."

Harry wiped his nose on a rag. "Nest, rest, that's not bad. But the meter's all wrong. Sorry, as a poet you're a flop."

"Your opinion is noted."

"Testy!" Harry said. "Edith, where is my supper? This fellow is too thick headed and irritating to be worth a man's conversation."

Edith smiled thinly. "Jennie will be out soon enough with your scraps. Now you keep quiet." She turned to Stephen, holding out a coil of rope. "Up with that shirt of yours then. We haven't any time to waste, young man, if you're dead set on doing this idiotic thing."

Stephen raised his shirt and she wrapped the rope around his middle, muttering repeatedly, "Stupid plan, really stupid plan."

When she was done, Stephen lowered his shirt, grateful for its protection against the chill, which had grown worse with the retreat of the sun, and checked the girth on the saddled mare. The other mare carried only extra blankets, for it would be cold during the night, and food.

"Makes you look fat," Harry said. "It won't fool anyone."

"Shut up, Harry," Gilbert said.

"Fool's idea," Edith said stepping back.

"Remember," Stephen said to Gilbert, "the western base of the north watchtower. I'll show no sooner than two hours after sundown."

"It'll be a damn cold night," Gilbert grumbled.

"I know. I'm sorry. Godspeed to you now because we won't have a chance to speak again." Stephen paused. "And thank you."

Gilbert nodded.

Stephen hurried out of the yard.

The warden at the castle gate was just closing its massive, single, iron-studded door when Stephen stumped across the wooden bridge spanning the ditch. The warden held the door cracked for him, then drove it closed and dropped the bar. "Cutting it close there, aren't you?" the warden asked.

"I forgot the hour, Ben," Stephen said.

Now that he was inside, Stephen could relax a bit. With the closing of the gate, it was Ben's time to knock off, so together they walked up the path toward the inner keep, leaving his replacement for the first watch to settle on his stool in the guard's niche.

"Got some late business with his lordship?" Ben asked, meaning Valence.

"Something like that, yes," Stephen said. He asked carefully as if he didn't care, although he was worried that

Valence might have had a sudden change of heart and left unexpectedly: "He's still here, isn't he?"

"Oh, yeah, unfortunately." But Ben brightened. "He went hunting this afternoon with Henle. They killed two deer. There'll be venison tonight. I might even get some."

"I hope you do."

"We hardly ever get good meat," Ben grumbled.

"It's the lot of all soldiers," Stephen said, "unless you kill it yourself."

"Wish I could. But when's a man like me going to get the chance to go hunting? Don't even own a bow, anyway."

"I've got one I'll lend you. But only for target practice, mind!"

Ben grinned. "I might take you up on that someday."

They passed through the tunnel-like passage to the inner bailey. Stephen angled toward the round chapel, which sat in the middle of the bailey to the right, while Ben continued straight across to the hall.

"You'll miss supper!" Ben said.

"Oh, I already ate. Besides, I feel the need of some absolution."

Ben laughed. "What have you been up to today?"

"Nothing good," Stephen said.

Ben waved and went into the hall.

Stephen went into the chapel.

As he expected, it was deserted.

He pulled the hood up over his head, for it was getting even colder, wrapped his cloak around himself, and sat with his back to the wall by the door to wait.

Stephen had planned to mark the passage of time in part by relying on the observation of Compline, which normally took place about an hour after sundown. But neither the chaplain nor anyone else came in for the service. Laughing, music and singing drifted across from the hall, where the usual evening entertainments were underway. They must be having an exceptionally good time and there must have been venison indeed at supper, which usually was a light meal, to keep the chaplain from his duty. Stephen glanced out the door for a glimpse of the stars so he could gauge the time that way, but the sky had clouded. He would have to guess the time, and he knew from having spent many a night on guard duty how time slowed down when it was dark, and how a quarter hour could seem like two whole ones.

After what seemed like forever, the music and voices faded in volume. He heard the footfalls of a few people retreating across the yard to the outer bailey and the subdued drone of their conversations — men and women, servants and soldiers on the way to bed. Two men paused by the chapel door and took a piss against the wall. They went away. There was a fluttering inside the chapel that startled Stephen. He thought he wasn't alone for a moment, but he couldn't see anyone. Then he realized it was bats flying in the upper reaches of the structure and through the door. Birds nested up there too, but they were asleep.

The foot traffic trickled out. There was a series of thuds as a warden shut and barred the gate to the outer bailey, sealing off the two parts of the castle from each other. Stephen had wondered if the watch still took this precaution. It would have made things much easier if they had grown slack. There were only two gates out of the castle, the main gate and a small sally port in the north wall, and both of them offered admittance only into the outer bailey. There was no way out of the inner bailey now.

He rose and crossed to the hall. There were lights behind the shutters signifying that a few people were still awake. In a few upper windows, some of the lights appeared to move — people with candles settling down to their beds.

He opened the right-hand door and entered. Largely empty now of people, the enormous room seemed more vast than it really was. The ceiling rose up three stories, an impossible distance. Sometimes children amused themselves when the adults weren't watching by trying to hit the rafters with balls, but they rarely succeeded, the distance was so great. Valence and Henle had gone to bed, of course, which was Stephen's main worry. He had no business being here after dark, and if they had seen him, it would have meant questions for which he had no good answers. One of the men-servants was putting out the last of the candles with a candle snuffer which was at the end of a long pole because the candle holders were on the sides of pillars a full eight or ten feet off the ground. The musicians were still on their stools putting away their instruments in boxes and little trunks and downing the last of their ale. Several women were bringing in straw pallets for the servants who slept in the hall. A dozen children of varying ages were running around playing tag; then a mother spoke sharply at them to quiet down, and with obvious sullenness and repressed rebellion, the children collected against a wall to wait till their beds were made.

Stephen wended through this organized confusion to the stairs which led upward to the apartments. Head down, masked in his cloak, he attracted no particular attention. These people, merely servants, would neither stop him nor call an alarm if they recognized him, which was a possibility. But he preferred not to be noticed or recognized. He was counting on the bedtime activity to conceal him.

The stairway was dark and he bumped into a woman whom he neither saw nor heard coming. "Watch it, love," she said, "or I'll knock you down."

"You nearly did," Stephen said with a forced laugh.

"Oh, sorry, sir," she said, realizing from his accent he was gentry. "I didn't see you."

"Nor I you," Stephen said. "No harm done." He went round her and continued his climb.

He made his way in the pitch dark to the very top of the stairs. He had to navigate by feel, but he was pleased to find that he remembered the way very well. He had been a page and squire here under Henle's predecessor in the days before his father had decided he needed a profession and sent him to London to be Valence's clerk. The room he was headed to had been his own; like the boys who inhabited it now, he had been thrown out to look for other accommodations when guests arrived.

At the top of the stairs, he went right exactly five steps, running his hand along the wall until it encountered the door. Despite his attempts at stealth, the wooden floors creaked and protested as they always had, a familiar sound that roused sad nostalgia. He had been happy here; not at first, of course, for the initial separation from his mother had been hard and the discipline had been strict. But he had grown to love it.

The door was closed and no light showed; nor had he expected it. He rapped the door three times and called through it, "Gunnora!" He had to repeat this several times, but finally was rewarded by rustling and thumping behind the door and it opened a crack.

"Who is it?" a woman asked.

Stephen could tell by her voice it was Gunnora, and he was relieved he had the right room. "It's me, Stephen."

"What are you doing here?" Gunnora asked, plainly surprised.

This was where he had to get rough, and he took no pleasure in it. But he wasn't sure whether she would resist and how much, whether she would call an alarm or remain silent. He had no claim on her loyalty or cooperation and he could not afford to take any chances. Stephen pushed open the door and grasped folds of Gunnora's nightgown. "If you say another word, I'll wring your neck," he snarled.

She stiffened in fright, but did not resist as he pushed her into the room and shut the door. With clouds covering the half-moon and the shutters closed, it was so dark in the room that he couldn't see his hand in front of his face. He had to find the bed by feel, but it was a small room and a large bed — big enough for four or five boys at once — and he collided with it only two steps inside the room. He forced Gunnora, who was rigid with fright, onto the bed.

"Turn over," he said.

She complied, trembling. She must think he intended to rape her.

He bound her hands and feet, firmly but not so tightly as to be uncomfortable. Then he rolled her over onto her back.

"I'm sorry, Gunnora," he said. "I don't want to hurt you. I'm going to have to gag you now." He removed a linen strip from his belt pouch.

"Just not too tightly, please."

"Of course."

He put the strip across her mouth and tied it behind her head, being as careful as he could not bind it in her long hair. Then he pulled her up so her head was on the pillow and threw the covers over her so she would not get cold.

Stephen located Christopher by his soft breathing. The boy was too big for a cradle now and lay on a small pallet on the floor beside the bed because he still wet himself at night.

"Cristofo!" Stephen whispered, picking up the little body. "*Es tu papa.*"

"*Papa! Que es?*" Christopher asked in his high-pitched child's voice.

"You must be quiet," Stephen continued in Spanish. "It's very important. You understand? We're going on a journey. Sit still." He put the boy on the edge of the bed and fumbled around for his clothes and shoes. He regretted now having gagged Gunnora, for she could have directed him, but there was only one trunk after all, and it held all the things he needed. It took only a few minutes to get the boy properly dressed against the rigors of the night.

"*Tengo sed,*" Christopher said.

"*Yo se, pero necessita esperar un poco.*"

"*Tengo sed,*" Christopher repeated. "*Quiero tomar.*"

"*Bueno. Pero esperate.*"

"*Quiero tomar,*" Christopher said matter of factly. Then he started babbling in a mixture of Spanish and English. Stephen shushed him, but the boy kept on until Stephen shoved his thumb in his mouth so he could suck it.

The boy on his hip, Stephen said to Gunnora, "We're going now. Give me an hour before you try to get free."

She couldn't answer, of course, so he couldn't tell if she agreed to give him the time.

He went out and closed the door softly.

On this floor there was a door that opened onto the northern wall walk. Stephen eased his head out and looked left and right. It was so dark he could barely see anything. Here, the walk was like a narrow alley, the walls of the hall pressing in from one side and the crenelations of the castle wall on the other. Drainage was bad at this spot and because it was one of those places in the castle not open to public view and was little visited by the steward, it was not well kept up. Puddles collected that seemed to last forever and spawned nasty unmentionable things; moss and lichen grew on stones and timbers which never saw the sun; and the whiff of decay hung in the still air. Stephen held his breath and listened. He heard no sound of breathing, no scrape of boot leather. No one was about. That was good.

He slipped out the door, stepping carefully and trying not to make any noise. Noise, especially noise made by men, always seemed to carry in the dark. He didn't know how much time he had before the watch made its rounds on this part of the walls. Sometimes, because of the treacherous footing on these stones, the watch didn't come here; or it hadn't when he was a boy and had to take his turns standing night guard. But he couldn't be sure that things hadn't changed under the castle's present master. You never knew.

Stephen put Christopher down. The boy tried to wander off and Stephen caught his arm and hissed for him to stand still. Then he unwound the rope from about his waist. He rubbed the irritated band it had left on his skin.

He wrapped one end of the rope around Christopher to form a harness. He had practiced this last night on Gilbert's young son, a boy of seven also named Gilbert though everyone called him Gillie, at the Broken Shield. But there had been light then, and now he had to do it in the dark and he was petrified that he had not got either the weave or the knot right. A mistake would mean the boy's death. He tested the harness by lifting the child up and letting him dangle and swing. Christopher thought this was a game and he cried out. Stephen put him down immediately and shushed him.

"Don't talk, don't say anything, don't make a noise," Stephen said.

Christopher laughed and grabbed him about the neck, still convinced they were playing a game.

Stephen realized that nothing he could say would make the boy be silent. The sound of a child's laughter and babble should be audible throughout the inner bailey and were unusual enough at this hour that someone might come to investigate soon.

Panic began to surge like a tide, carrying the thought, like flotsam, that he had to gag Christopher. It seemed like a cruel thing to do. But he didn't think he had any choice. He had nothing to use for a gag. With his dagger, he cut a strip from the hem of his shirt.

Christopher didn't take well to the gag. Gagging was not part of any game he knew and he struggled while Stephen put it in place.

Christopher began to cry.

The gag didn't do much to muffle the sound.

Stephen had to hurry.

He climbed between two crenelations and lifted Christopher like he was a sack of grain being unloaded from a ship.

Then he swung him over the dark abyss outside the walls.

Christopher began to struggle.

To his horror, Stephen saw the boy was trying to get free — and succeeding. In moments he would squirm his way out of the harness. It was a good thirty feet to the ground and if he fell, he would die.

Stephen let the rope run fast through his hands. It burned and he wished he had thought to bring gloves.

Then, finally, the rope went slack and Gilbert called from below, "I've got him!" Then he said more faintly, "Hush, boy. That's a good boy."

Stephen dropped the rope into the outer dark.

It was done.

Christopher was safe. Valence wouldn't be able to touch him now.

He felt enormous relief.

The door to the big square tower only a few feet to the right opened and a warden stepped out.

"What the devil do you think you're doing?" the warden demanded.

"Taking a piss," Stephen said.

"That's the stupidest place to pee I ever saw, you idiot. Don't you know there's a latrine just inside the tower?"

"No." Stephen hopped down onto the wall walk.

The warden grunted. He leaned close and sniffed Stephen's breath to see how much he'd been drinking. "Well, you're not the first fool to make water that way. Had a fellow fall doing it last year. Landed on his head, he did. Drove it right into the ground like a nail."

"Ow," Stephen said with a grimace.

"I doubt he felt a thing, drunken bastard. What was all that racket?"

"Some woman walking a baby. She said he couldn't sleep. Fussy brat."

"They all are. Well, good night."

"G'night."

The warden stepped back into the tower and shut the door.

Chapter 14

Stephen descended to the hall and commandeered the lord's high-backed chair with its thick pillow cushion, which he set before the dying embers of the fire to await developments. He thought he might at least be warm and comfortable before all hell broke loose.

There was always something soothing about halls at night and this one was no exception — the fire burning low, shedding a fading orange glow, and gentle noises in the dark. Most everyone in the hall was asleep by now, except for a few coupling couples who made rhythmic noises in the dark. There was the occasional cough, a sneeze or two, a mother shushing a troubled child, a muttered rebuke at someone claiming more than his share of the blanket. All was easy and peaceful.

At long last there was commotion upstairs, voices raised, and the distant rumble of running feet. Gunnora, it seemed, was a fair judge of time, for it felt as though far more than an hour had passed, which meant that probably half of one had gone by.

Eventually, the thunder of feet reached the stairs and clamored down to the hall. Figures shouting and bearing candles fanned out and roused those who had been sleeping. One tall figure, stork-like despite his billowing nightshirt and woolen cloak, stalked to the hearth. He regarded the embers, hand on his hip. Then he turned to see who sat in his chair.

Valence's mouth opened in what seemed intended to be a snarl to frighten away the interloper, but then snapped shut. He bent to see if Stephen was really Stephen. So close their noses almost touched, Valence asked, "What have you done with him?"

Stephen flipped his hand dismissively, although the gesture cost him. He was frightened of Valence, of the power and influence the man wielded and the retribution he could call down like lightning. Stephen was no fool: he had learned long ago that it was wise for the powerless to fear the powerful. Although the law was supposed to afford protection, in practice many powerful men just ignored it and did what they pleased simply because there was no one who could make them answer for what they did. Sometimes, though, one's best protection was boldness. He said: "That is none of your business, your honor."

Valence straightened up. He was breathing hard. A cheek muscle twitched — familiar signs of a tantrum over the horizon. But the eruption did not come. Valence controlled himself. "I had only offered him my protection. I was only concerned with his welfare."

They both knew this was untrue, but Stephen gained nothing by making that understanding public and increasing Valence's embarrassment, which was already substantial. He said, "It seemed, in my judgment, that a change of situation was needed."

"You had only to ask," Valence said. He was recovering quickly.

Stephen almost laughed at the absurdity of the claim. He said smoothly, "I am afraid I am rather rash at times. My apologies if this inconvenienced you." He stood up. "I see I've taken your chair, your honor. My apologies again for my presumptuousness."

Valence sat down. He called over his shoulder, "Clement, you can stop looking! The brat isn't here!" He returned his attention to Stephen. "Why aren't you gone too?"

Stephen shrugged. "I gave my word I'd find your list. I don't need a knife at my throat to force me to do it."

"A knife at your throat, my boy, whatever gave you the impression I was trying to coerce you?"

"I was speaking figuratively, your honor."

"Ah, indeed." Valence steepled his hands. He was surprised but pleased with this development. "Have you made any progress?"

"I would make more if Clement didn't interfere."

"What are you saying? Clement? What's he done?"

"It seems he's making his own inquiries. He bashed the face in of the mother of the prime suspect — who may know where this man is hiding. Now she's unable to talk to me, and even if she could I think Clement's so frightened her that she would say nothing."

Valence barked over his shoulder, "Clement! Come here!"

After a few moments, Clement's square, solid figure emerged from the pool of dark surrounding the hearth. Behind him people were blowing out candles and going back to bed. "Yes, my lord?" he asked warily, having sensed Valence's wrath in his tone.

"What have you been up to?" Valence asked with silky menace.

Clement's eyes flicked from Valence to Stephen and back again. "Nothing, my lord."

"Don't take me for a fool, Clement. You've been asking questions of your own, haven't you."

Clement hesitated. "Yes, sir. Just looking out for your interests, sir. You can't depend on him alone to help you."

"How very thoughtful. I had no idea you had a talent or an interest in investigation. That's all to the good. Two noses on the trail will get results twice as fast. Well, then, what have you found out?"

"In front of him?" Clement asked, gesturing to Stephen.

"Yes. Share with us what you've learned. No reason for us to keep secrets from one another. We all want the same thing."

"Can't say as I've learned a lot, sir. Unfortunately."

"Oh. Too bad. What's this about a woman, bashed her face in, something like that?"

"That would be Makepeese's mother," Clement said warily. "I didn't bash her face in. She came at me with an axe. Wanted to chop my head off. Crazy woman. I was just defending myself. I can't help it if she got hurt."

"Yes, yes, but did she tell you anything useful?"

"No. She's covering up for Makepeese, I'm sure. She always hated me. Wouldn't tell me a thing. I think you'd learn more if you had her arrested and questioned her proper."

"You really think so?"

"I do, sir."

Valence steepled his hands again. His rings, which he evidently wore even to bed for them to be on display now, seemed to wobble on stick-like fingers. "Very well. See that it's done. Speak to the clerk. He'll draw up the necessary writ."

"Very good, sir." Clement grinned wolfishly at Stephen and withdrew into the dark. His footsteps came heavily on the stairs.

"How's your back?" Valence asked Stephen.

"It's fine."

"The scars still there?" Years ago, Valence had had Stephen savagely caned for what had seemed a trivial misdemeanor. The beating was the reason Stephen had run away from his apprenticeship.

"They've faded. They're not noticeable any longer."

"That's good." Valence rose and slid his bony hands into the sleeves of his nightshirt. "If you succeed instead of Clement, I will forgive this outrage. If not . . . well, the king will be displeased at your failure . . . it could show a certain lack of loyalty, don't you think? They say his rages are terrible." He shrugged. "Good night, Stephen. Enjoy the competition."

"Good night, your honor."

Now that he had had his talk with Valence, there was no longer any reason to remain in the castle. Although the wardens weren't supposed to let anyone in or out after sundown, that rule was relaxed for men claiming to be on the king's business. It was too bad that Stephen couldn't have walked out with Christopher in his arms, as he did now. But the wardens had been under orders to ensure the boy remained inside.

The main gate shut with a double thud: the closing of the door and the falling of the bar. Stephen's footsteps on the wooden bridge over the castle's outer ditch thumped hollowly in the night and then crunched on the dirt of High Street. The houses bordering the broad street, which in daylight rose tall and proud, were like the silhouettes of mountains in the grim dark.

He walked swiftly down High Street, head down and lost in thought, considering what he knew. It wasn't much. He was convinced that William Muryet, the murdered butler, and Howard Makepeese had conspired to steal the list, although he couldn't know that for certain. He still thought that the most plausible explanation was that they had fallen out and Makepeese had killed Muryet to acquire the list or all the money for himself. Yet if Lucy knew where Makepeese was, it meant he had gone into hiding somewhere nearby and had not fled as any murderer would be expected to. That must mean that he still had the list and had not sold it yet — had not sold it because he was waiting for the buyer.

All he had to do was find Lucy and wring the truth from her. Before Clement found out about her.

With that thought in his head, he paused at the mouth of College Lane. He considered whether to roust her now in the night. She had not been at the Baynard house when he had left in the evening, but she was sure to have returned.

He was about to turn down College Lane when he caught the whiff of a sound behind him. A slow sound, a stealthy sound. The faint grind of shoe leather on a pocket of gravel.

Someone was following him.

He went round the corner and stopped. Ducking low so that his head was no higher than the tops of his boots and less likely to be seen, he looked back around the corner. A shadow detached itself from that of a house down the street. It was a small shadow belonging to a boy, but Stephen could make out nothing about him. He waited. There was the sound of running footsteps. The boy peeked around the corner. Stephen grabbed him.

This close, Stephen knew who it was: the same boy he'd seen loitering outside St. Laurence's the other day; the same boy who'd been with the men who'd attacked him outside the Broken Shield. "Got you," Stephen said, giving the boy a rough shake. "Who sent you?"

The boy did not reply. A hand came out from behind his back. It held a dagger. He thrust at Stephen's stomach.

Stephen pushed him away and backed up to gain space. Even boys with daggers were as dangerous as grown men.

The boy backed up too. He did not run away. He didn't seem frightened of Stephen at all. He calmly held the dagger at his hip where it stood ready to strike and could not be grabbed. He clearly knew how to use it.

"Who are you working for, boy?" Stephen asked.

"Fuck if I'll tell you," the boy said.

"Fair enough, I suppose, in answer to just a question. But I'll give you tuppence if you tell me."

The boy laughed. "What rot. You ain't got tuppence. What that blonde lady sees in a poor fart like you I don't know."

The reply startled Stephen. The boy must have been following him all day. At least he might think Stephen was going back to Baynard House to see Margaret.

But he was not going there to see Margaret.

He decided not to go there at all tonight. Lucy would be at Baynard House in the morning. Besides, there was somewhere else he needed to go. Lucy could wait till morning. This could not.

But before he went there he had to lose the tail.

Stephen edged around the boy, who pivoted to face him, then strode off fast across High Street to Broad. As he descended Broad Street he heard the boy behind him, who was no longer trying to remain invisible. All to the good.

He turned into Bell Lane. He glanced backward. The boy was still there, a faint silhouette at the mouth of the street.

The front door to the Broken Shield was barred, of course, as was the gate to the yard. Stephen leaped to the top of the wall and pulled himself up and over. He dropped into the yard, stifling a yelp of pain from his bad foot, which did not like the impact.

Then he ran past the stables to the rear fence, which he climbed just as nimbly.

He found himself in a grove of cherry and peach trees in the neighbor's back garden. A stack of firewood taller than he was and almost reached the height of the fence stood to the left. The stench of a latrine was strong, which meant it was nearby, although he couldn't see it. The last thing he wanted was to fall in, least of all because of the possibility of getting filthy. Some latrine pits were so deep that people were known to drown in them after falling in at night.

This garden was also home to at least three large, noisy dogs. They lived in a shed on the other side of the woodpile. Stephen waited nervously for them to start to howl, worried it would alert his young tail that he was going out the back door. But the dogs must have been sleeping, because there was no sound of alarm.

Gingerly, Stephen made his way through the grove to the other side of the yard, which also was bordered by a high fence.

He climbed that one too and dropped into the alley that ran between two yards, opening on the left onto Broad Street.

At the corner, he peeked around to make sure the tail did not have Broad Street under surveillance. In the dark it was impossible to tell. Stephen just had to take the chance.

Keeping next to the houses, he scurried down the hill to Broad Gate.

He found Gip the warden asleep in his niche by the door. Going inside, Stephen prodded Gip with his good foot.

"Whoa, what is it?" Gip sputtered, coming awake.

"I need you to open the gate," Stephen said. "I'm going out."

"Got your penny?"

"This is king's business."

"King's business, my ass. You're on a doxy hunt."

"Believe me or not, but put it on my tab, if you must."

"I don't run tabs, lad."

"You'll run one tonight, or it'll be your ass indeed."

"Easy, easy, I was just having some fun."

"So was I."

"Fair enough, fair enough."

Gip grumpily opened the gate just enough for Stephen to slip through.

"Sleep tight, old man," Stephen said.

"I would if it weren't for young farts like you." He pushed the gate shut.

Instead of continuing down Broad Street, Stephen clambered into the ditch that ran around the town at the base of the wall. It was as good as any street for where he wanted to go now. He moved a little less quickly and without quite so much stealth. It was very doubtful the boy would get past Gip if he realized Stephen had left the town.

Before long, he reached and crossed under the footbridge at Old Street, where a sally port ran out of Ludlow from the southeast. He stayed in the ditch, skirting piles of trash that people had dumped there. It was against the law to throw trash in the ditch, but people did it anyway.

Soon he came to Galdeford Gate on the east side of town. He clambered up to the street and took the left fork in the road, counting the houses as he went. Before long, the little chapel loomed in the dark, and beyond it the large spreading oak. He crossed the ditch on the plank bridge and went into the Makepeeses' yard. The house was silent, but the glimmer of a fire showed through cracks in the door. Stephen wondered if the old crone was still awake.

He rapped on the door. The thuds seemed unnaturally loud in the quiet of the night.

After a few moments, the old crone's voice came through the door. "Who is it?"

"Stephen Attebrook, the deputy coroner."

"What the hell do you want?"

"Crack the door and I'll tell you."

The old crone was some time making up her mind, but eventually the door eased open a crack to reveal one eye and a sliver of her face. "All right, talk. But don't think about coming in. I'll gut you sure if you try it."

Stephen laughed. "You'll be the third person tonight who's wanted to. But I'll remain where I am, so rest easy. Now listen. Clement's coming back to arrest Mistress Makepeese. He's to take her to the castle for more questioning, and you can guess what kind that'll be."

"The screw and the rack!" the old woman spat.

"Right. So you've got to get her out of here. The sooner the better."

"She can't move and I've not the strength to carry her."

"Have you got a place for her and the children to hide, at least for a few days?"

"I've a hut across that field."

What field she meant he couldn't tell. He said, "I'll carry her then. Get the kids up."

The old woman stepped back and Stephen entered the house.

Mistress Makepeese looked fearfully up at him from her pallet.

The old woman said, "It's all right, Beth. He's come to warn us Clement's on his way."

Beth Makepeese made a frightened moan.

"We'll go to my house," the old woman said. "He'll carry you." She called up into the loft. "Sally! Get Edward and the others up. Right away. We have to go now. Hurry!"

Stephen kicked dirt on the fire to put it out while the children clambered down from the loft, clutching a few odds and ends of belongings.

Suddenly Sally, the oldest girl, said, "I hear horses — more than one, on the road coming from town."

Stephen strained to listen. At first he heard nothing. Then he caught the faint thudding of horses' hooves. They had to be close — right outside the front gate. The sound stopped. A man's voice carried across the yard. Clement hadn't waited for morning after all.

"Get them out the back — now!" he hissed. "They're right out front."

He scooped up Beth Makepeese as the old woman ushered the children out the back door. With Beth on one arm, he closed the back door softly behind him, just as the front door gave way with a crash.

Chapter 15

The children and the old woman were out of sight. Only the rustle of their footsteps in the grass gave evidence of their presence, and soon that faded to nothing.

Beth Makepeese was not a large woman, but she felt like three sacks of grain. There was no chance he could take the same route as the others and hope to be out of sight before Clement or one of his companions thought to open the back door.

Stephen turned left and lumbered toward the corner of the house. Inside, the men rattled around, cursing. Someone threw open the shutters of a window just as he passed. Stephen froze against the house, clutching a trembling Beth, not daring to breathe. If the man stuck his head out . . .

But apparently he did not, for there was no cry of alarm.

Stephen dared to move again. He slithered to the corner of the house and glanced around it. No man-shape moved there. He thought it was safe enough and reeled across the open ground to a lean-to that stood about twenty feet away, visible as only a black blob in the greater dark. As he reached the lean-to, two men came round the side of the house. Stephen, standing in the open, froze again. If he didn't move, they might mistake him for a tree or a post. As an experienced hunter, he knew that motion betrayed the target, which might remain unseen if it was still.

The two men went past into the rear yard. Stephen eased behind the lean-to. "There's no one here!" one of the men called.

Clement emerged from the back door and kicked a bucket that Stephen must have just missed in his flight. It clattered off into the dark, unseen. "Shit!" he snarled. "Shit and damnation!"

"Where do you suppose they went?"

"I don't know," Clement said angrily, "but it ain't right. Somebody's warned them we were coming. I'm sure of it."

"But who?"

"Attebrook," Clement spat. "It had to be him. He's the only one who knew."

"There's one way to find out. See if he's at the Shield."

"We'll do that, but I've had a tail on him for the last couple of days. They'll know what he's been up to." Clement stalked round the house. "Let's go, boys. We've another house call to make."

When they had gone, Stephen put Beth down so he could rest a moment. Now that he could breathe freely, he could not seem to catch his breath and his arms felt like they were made of string. Beth sank to the ground and began to cry, but it seemed more with relief now than from fright.

"It's all right, Beth," he said. "They're gone."

"El buh bah," she said several times. It took a few moments before Stephen realized she was saying, "They'll be back."

"Yes, but you won't be here."

Still crying, she blubbered, "Nah safe ever."

Stephen knelt beside her, his face close to her's. "You'll never be safe as long as Clement thinks you have the list. You know about the list, don't you?"

Beth's crying subsided, but she said nothing. Finally, she nodded.

"Howard took it, didn't he," Stephen said.

"Yeah."

"He and Muryet."

She nodded again.

"Where is it?"

"Don' kno'." Don't know.

"Does Howard have it?"

"Don' kno'!"

"Where is Howard?"

She shook her head. "Di'n nev-uh tell uh wheah he's going." He didn't never tell us where he's going.

"But Lucy knows."

Beth nodded.

"How does Lucy know?"

"She luh heah." She loves him. "He sayuh i'ah make uh rish." He said it would make us rich.

"He was wrong. It will be your death. Did Howard kill Muryet?"

"Duh nuh. He di'ah cum ba-ah tha' nigh'." He didn't come back that night.

It was clear Stephen wouldn't learn anything more that might be useful, but what he had learned brought him much closer than he had been half an hour ago. He now knew for sure that Howard Makepeese had taken the list — that was now fact and not an educated guess. Since he was in hiding, he probably still had it. All Stephen had to do was find Howard, and this ordeal would be over.

"Where did they go?" meaning the old woman and the children.

"Tha way." Beth pointed across the field to the rear of the house.

"Let's go find them, then."

Stephen hoisted her on his back and began the long trod across the field toward the black woods beyond.

Chapter 16

The morning was shrouded with fog when Stephen emerged from the crone's hut in the woods. He was glad to be up and about, even though he was dead tired. He hadn't slept much during the night. It was a small hut, barely big enough for two people, and had been asked to hold eight. It had been so crowded that Stephen had had no place to stretch out and had ended up sitting against a wall. He had slept under worse conditions — there had been a few memorable times when he'd slept on horseback and once he'd even fallen asleep while standing guard on a castle wall. But one of the children had trod on his hand during the night on her way to relieve herself and the pain had kept him awake a long time afterward. His fingers still smarted.

The fog was thick and soupy and filled the air with a metallic scent. He could barely see fifty yards and the sun didn't show through, so he had no idea what time it was.

He had to find Lucy right away.

Because of the fog, he couldn't get his bearings and had no idea which way to go. Fortunately, the crone, who's name was Julia, emerged. "Fetch me some firewood, would you, lad?" she asked. "My poor old back is smarting."

"I've business," he said impatiently. "Which way's the town?"

"Business, have you? Too proud for a little honest work, eh? Well," she pointed to the left, "it's that way, cross the field. When you hit the road you'll be able to find your way easily enough."

"Thank you." Stephen hoped she was telling the truth. He'd been sent in the wrong direction before by people pretending to be helpful. Nevertheless, despite his urgent desire to be on his way, he tarried a few moments to gather an armful of firewood from the pile behind the house, which he put inside the door for Julia.

"You're a good boy," Julia cackled. "You do your mother proud."

"I always was her favorite son," he said. "That led to the trouble."

"What trouble?"

"Never mind. Good day to you, and take care of Helen. I'll let you know when it's safe for her to go back to her house."

Julia nodded. "Go with God."

"That sounds funny coming from a witch."

"That's what you think I am?"

"It seems obvious."

Julia smiled crookedly with a shred of mocking malice. "God is no enemy of witches, I'll have you know, whatever most people think. Now get out of here, before I put a curse on you!"

She said the last with emphasis, and watched him closely to gauge his reaction, as if hoping he would be frightened; she seemed set to enjoy that prospect. But he only bowed slightly and turned away, unmoved by her threat. "Witches have their place in the world too!" she called to his back. "We know more about healing than most physicians!"

"I've no doubt of that!" Stephen called to the fog. "Next time I have a palsy I'll consult you!"

"Do that!" she called, her voice already muffled by distance. "There's only a slight chance you may die!"

Stephen grinned to himself and walked faster.

It must have been a good quarter mile to the road, and by the time he found it, his boots were sopping with dew and caked with dirt from the field. He eased over the wattle fence, leaped the ditch, and stood in the middle of the road, trying to get his bearings. The fog had thinned a bit and he could see a hundred yards now. That lump to the right had to be Helen Makepeese's house. While he stood there, a pair of one-horse carts lumbered out of the fog. They were loaded with sacks of freshly threshed grain, no doubt on their way to one of the water mills on the river. The lead driver greeted him with a curse for blocking the way. Stephen dodged back to the lip of the ditch to let them pass.

He hurried after the carts. As he got closer to town, foot and cart traffic increased. He guessed from its volume that it must be at least an hour after sunrise, although the fog was so thick you'd never know there was a sun at all. Stephen grew increasingly worried. If Lucy loved Howard, Clement had to know it. They had been members of the same household and both done Baynard's dirty work. Unable to question Helen Makepeese further, he would undoubtedly seize Lucy next and wring from her the secret of Howard's hiding place.

By the time Stephen reached Galdeford Gate, the carts had taken the road south around the town, and the fog had begun to burn off. Patches of bright blue sky were intermittently visible. It was late indeed.

Stephen pressed through a small throng at the gate. The warden, a man just out of boyhood who didn't know him, snatched at Stephen's arm, demanding the toll. Stephen shook him off. He began to run. His feet just started to move on their own. For a grown man to run full tilt through the town was a shocking breach of protocol. Grown men, particularly crown officials, were expected to act with dignity. Running was for thieves and other wrong-doers. But he couldn't help it. Several townsfolk took after him, thinking he was trying to evade the toll, but as Stephen reached Beasts' Market, they fell away, for others had recognized him and called them off. Heads swivelled to follow his progress, however, and tongues were surely wagging. Before dinner, everyone in town would know he had been acting strangely again. He wondered how long it would be before complaints about him reached Sir Geoff's ears, and what Sir Geoff would do about them.

He slowed as he turned up College Lane, panting to catch his breath before he reached Baynard House. He was determined not to present himself in such a harried state. It was bad enough that he needed a bath, a hair combing, and a change of clothes.

A girl who was not Lucy answered his knock and admitted him into the entranceway. He asked after Lucy, trying hard not to sound alarmed or worried. The girl looked apologetic, but before she could respond, Margaret rushed in from the hall. She must have heard his voice.

She dismissed the young maid and took his arm urgently. "Stephen, you're just in time."

"What's happening?"

"She's gone out, no more than a quarter hour ago."

Stephen was appalled. Clement could simply snatch her off the street. A girl as frail as Lucy wouldn't survive under torture. She'd die before anyone would know she had been taken. "You didn't try to detain her?"

"No, why would I? But I think she's up to something. She went out with a large basket full of food!" She lowered her voice to a whisper. "I think she's going to see him!"

Stephen must have looked skeptical because Margaret added, "Why else would she go out wearing stout walking shoes and cloaked against the weather?"

Stephen nodded thoughtfully. It seemed reasonable. "But we've no idea where she's gone."

Margaret looked proud of herself. "I've sent my men after her. I told one to return with news of which road she's taken."

"Well done. I suppose we've only to wait for him."

"Not here. I'll get my cloak. We'll wait at the corner."

They emerged to see one of Margaret's grooms walking fast toward them. He gave Stephen a cold, measured stare, then turned to Margaret with a slight bow. "My lady," he said, "the girl left town by that south gate."

"Broad Gate," Stephen interjected.

"I believe that's what you call it," the groom said.

"Where's James?" Margaret asked in a surprisingly businesslike tone.

"He stayed with her."

"Thank you, Walter," Margaret said. She turned to Stephen, "We must hurry if we're to catch up."

Stephen nodded grimly. He felt keenly that Lucy needed protection, as much as he wanted to learn what she knew, and that Margaret's groom James would not be enough. "It may be a long way. You'll want horses."

"Walter," Margaret said, "saddle three horses — the gelding for Sir Stephen and the two mares, and bring the mounts to us. We'll start on foot."

It was amazing how well she read his thoughts: she was as eager to be gone as he was and wasn't willing to wait for the horses to be saddled, for by then they might lose the trail.

They set off at a fast walk over High Street and down the long incline of Broad to the gate at the bottom. Stephen was glad to see that Harry had recovered enough from his fever to return to work, for there he was at his place by the gate, his begging cup on the ground before the exposed stumps of his legs, with several farthings and half-pennies already at the bottom.

Stephen intended to pause only a moment. "Harry, did Lucy Waps pass by this morning?"

"Could be that I have seen her, could be not," Harry said, stroking his ample beard and swirling the coins in his cup.

"This is urgent. I haven't time to argue."

"Don't know," Harry said. "Memory's kind of foggy. Fever does that to a man."

"Do you know this person?" Margaret asked sharply.

"Unfortunately, yes," Stephen said.

"Well, then." She dug in her purse and dropped a full penny in the cup. "Has this improved your memory?"

"You certainly know how to pick your friends, Sir Steve," Harry said. "I was wrong about you." He bowed, bringing his forehead down to his stumps and straightened up. "Seems as I have seen Miss Waps this morning. She passed by only a quarter hour ago."

Stephen said, "Did you see which way she went?"

Harry seemed about to hold out for additional money, but a penny was an awful lot of charity, a fact that registered on Margaret's face. "My lady," he said with uncharacteristic humility, "I saw her reach the foot of the bridge, but as you can see, beyond that my view is blocked."

Stephen glanced through the gate. Harry was right. The road bent right as it approached the bridge and the houses along the way blocked the view of the bridge and the other side of the river.

"Seems as I recall Miss Waps as well," Gip the gate warden said. "And I've a better view of the other side than our short friend here."

"Do you now," Stephen said, suspicious that Gip was just angling for his own penny.

"I would be very grateful if you told us which way she went," Margaret said.

Gip's hand twitched as if he was about to extend it, but Harry struck his calf. Gip glanced at Harry in irritation, then said, "I think she took the right fork across the bridge, but can't say as I was watching too close where she was going, if you know what I mean, me being a busy man and all."

"Of course," Margaret said. "Thank you. Stephen? Shall we?"

"Yes," Stephen said.

They passed through Broad Gate and hurried down to the river.

There were actually three forks in the road across the bridge. One led east along the riverbank, one mounted the hill to Ludford, and the other turned west toward Whitcliffe. Stephen hoped that by "right fork" Harry had meant the road to Whitcliffe. It was a gamble, but fortunately they came across a wagon with a broken axle no more than two hundred yards after the fork. The carter confirmed that a woman of Lucy's description had passed by only a short while before.

A quarter hour's head start put them almost a mile behind Lucy. It was an impossible distance to close on foot, and even if they had horses there was no guarantee they'd find her. She could turn down any little path and they might have no clue.

Stephen was beginning to think that the wiser course was to return to Broad Gate and set up a watch for Lucy's return when Walter cantered up with the horses he had been sent to fetch. The urgency of the pursuit had taken hold of him and with the appearance of the horses, he was unable to force himself to go back. He contented himself with asking Walter to station himself at Broad Gate instead. Walter glanced at Margaret who nodded.

Stephen boosted her onto the mare, and climbed aboard the gelding. He took the reins of the second mare, leaving Walter to walk back to town.

He squeezed the gelding's sides and gave rein. The gelding was warmed up and leaped into a canter with this negligible encouragement. Margaret came abreast of him and they rode easily together. The wind pulled her wimple back, revealing her forehead and strands of her hair. A flushed, pleased smile showed that she was enjoying herself, as if the urgency of their errand was forgotten.

The road followed the northward bend in the Teme for almost half a mile as it climbed up Whitcliffe hill, then turned west, then southwest and entered a wood. The road here was more a cart track than a proper road, three paths through the trees: two worn by carts' wheels and the center one by the horse. Stephen rode in one wheel path and Margaret rode in the other. Branches from the forest, which pressed in close, occasionally whipped their faces, and Stephen sometimes had to hold up a hand for protection. The road continued a steep climb through the wood. The gelding began to breathe heavily from the exertion and to slow down. Abruptly Margaret raised a warning hand and reined to a halt. Stephen stopped too. Ahead was the figure of a man walking in one of the wheel paths.

"That's James," Margaret said. "Lucy will not be far ahead."

"If she's still there."

"She should be. James is very —" She seemed to catch herself and said, "I instructed him to be careful."

They walked the horses now. Their hooves made low, muffled thumps on the dirt and swirled fallen leaves, gentle sounds swallowed by the forest. It wasn't long before they had caught up with James, who like Walter was a square, hard-looking man.

"Is she there?" Stephen asked. Although he peered up the road, he saw no sign of Lucy.

James nodded. "She's there, all right. I've let her get a little ahead. Do you want to take her now, sir?"

"No, I think we'll follow her. If she's as much in love with him as his mother is, she won't tell us a thing. I'll take over now. You hang back. We'll switch places in a little while."

"Very good, sir."

Stephen slid off the gelding and handed James the reins. He pulled the hood of his cloak over his head and hurried up the road. It was some time before a small, also-cloaked figure came into view. He could tell it was Lucy because she had her hood down and her hair, thick and brown, hung down her back in a single rope held together by a succession of blue ribbons, and she had a large wicker basket hanging from one shoulder. He hung back a couple of hundred yards, shuffling along and trying hard not to be noticeable. Now he had her, hunger replaced his anxiety: he hadn't eaten a full meal since day before yesterday, and he felt as though he had a rat in his stomach gnawing to get out. He pushed the sensation aside. It was a familiar feeling. He was used to being hungry. On campaign, they had sometimes gone four or five days without food. You just had to put up with it and keep going.

The road topped a rise and started its descent toward Aston and, in the farther distance, Adforton. Lucy reached a collection of three houses that stood to one side of the road in clearings hacked out of the forest. She stopped. Stephen jumped off the road just in time to avoid being seen. He lay down and looked around the base of an elm. Lucy was taking a drink from the well. Then she had conversation with a woman who was hanging laundry on a rope strung between two trees. The woman laughed at something Lucy said.

When Lucy continued on her way, Stephen got up and followed her. The woman hanging her wash gave him a hard look when he passed. So did a man with an axe who came out of one of the houses. Stephen hoped he only meant the axe for firewood. Suspicious lot, the English peasant.

The road continued to fall toward Aston, the ground rising to hills on either side which were visible now that the leaves had fallen. A quarter mile beyond the hamlet, the road widened from a track to a proper road. Someone was doing his duty in keeping up the road here. Lucy gave him a start when she stopped to take a pebble out of one of her shoes. Stephen slowed and kept coming. It would have looked suspicious if he had stopped and there hadn't been time to duck off the road, for he had made the mistake in walking in the middle. He cursed himself for being careless. Fortunately he reached a path coming in from the right and took that as if it was a perfectly natural thing to do. Crouching down, he could see Lucy through the screen of trees. She put on her shoe and turned away. Stephen sighed with relief and came out of the woods.

The land began to fall away less steeply, signaling that Aston was near. As suddenly as if cut with a knife the woods gave way to fields on either side filled with stubble from the autumn mowing. Without pause, Lucy continued her march, while Stephen worried about being exposed in this open country, which gave him nowhere to hide if she looked back. His only choice seemed to be to let her get farther ahead, and he was waiting at the edge of the wood when Margaret and James caught up.

"Should we change now, sir?" James asked.

"No. I'll keep on her," Stephen said. It probably was a good idea to change places, but he felt better when he had her in view. If he let James take over, he'd worry himself ragged.

Aston village was visible in the distance. Stephen let Lucy nearly reach it before he started after her, which now put a quarter mile between them. When she had disappeared among the houses, Stephen almost broke into a run, worried that she might turn off the road there, unseen. As he reached the other side of the village, he saw her on the road ahead, turning onto a side road that came in from the right.

He keenly felt the need to get closer now. He hadn't been in this part of the county in a long time, but if memory served, there was a forest up that road, and he didn't want to lose her in it. A stone's throw to the right, a tree-lined stream brushed the edge of the village and meandered southwestward, while the road out of the village ran to the southeast. If he followed the stream rather than the main road, it was a shorter distance to the path Lucy had taken. Stephen decided to follow the stream. He waved at Walter and Margaret to continue along the road to the crossroads. Margaret waved back that she understood.

The side road crossed the stream without benefit of a bridge, dipping into the water and rising on the other side. But it was a small stream and Stephen was able to jump across it, although it was clear by Lucy's muddy footprints that she had simply waded through it.

Lucy herself was not in view, but that was no surprise, since after this road crossed a narrow field, the wood ahead closed in again, tall, gray and somber, filled with the sadness of autumn.

Now that he was in the wood and she had not yet come in sight, he ran to catch up. The further he went, the more alarmed he became, because there was no Lucy. He must have run another quarter mile, and still there was no sight of her. He slowed to a walk.

Ahead, a party on horses trotted into view — a man and three gentry women accompanied by servants.

Stephen waved at the man and called in French, "Pardon me but could you help me?"

The party reined up. The gentry man looked him up and down skeptically with that arrogant measuring glance that was so typical of a man of his class. At last the man decided to speak. "And how may I help you?"

Stephen harbored secret satisfaction that his French was better than this fellow's. In some small way, it made up for his rather shabby appearance. "Did you pass a young girl, green cloak and a basket on her arm, by any chance?"

"No, we haven't seen any such person today."

"*Merci*," Stephen said, aghast.

Lucy had left the road.

"Is there some trouble afoot?" the man asked.

"Not exactly," Stephen said, "but I must find her."

The man snorted. "Well, good luck." He heeled his horse, and he and his women and servants trotted off toward Aston.

Stephen watched them go, suddenly sick. The horses were obliterating any footprints Lucy had left, destroying any chance he had of tracking her, which he should have been doing in the first place. He cursed himself for his overconfidence.

Feeling foolish, he headed back toward Aston himself. It wasn't long before he found Margaret and James. Margaret was in conversation with the man and women who had passed him earlier. Stephen felt like hanging back, but she saw him and beckoned. There was no escape.

When he reached the group, Margaret said, "Cecil, have you had speech with Sir Stephen? I see you've passed him, but perhaps you haven't been properly introduced."

"We spoke," the man Cecil said coolly, "but of introductions, no. We did not take the time for them, unfortunately."

"Well, may I present my good friend Stephen Attebrook. He's deputy coroner at Ludlow. Stephen, this is Cecil Marlbrook."

Stephen bowed slightly. Marlbrook returned the courtesy.

"Your horse gone lame?" Marlbrook asked. It was a reasonable enough question, since James, who was obviously a servant, had a mount, but Stephen did not.

Margaret answered for him, though, as if in an attempt to save him from the embarrassment of having to make up some lie. "We're investigating a murder."

Cecil blinked in surprise. It was hardly the answer he was expecting. "The girl he asked about is a murderer?"

"She's an important witness."

Marlbrook did not seem to care much. "As I said, we didn't see anyone like her." Cecil played with his gloves. They were expensive calf skin and finely tailored. "Gone up in smoke, it appears." He fixed his eyes on Margaret. "Will you be coming round for Christmas this year? Mother was asking after you."

"I may," Margaret laughed.

After a few more minutes of polite conversation while Stephen chafed, Marlbrook took his leave.

"They are friends, Stephen," Margaret said at the look on Stephen's face. "I couldn't ignore them."

"I know you couldn't. But I can't tell where Lucy's gone now, and with every passing moment, she gets farther away."

"Well, if Cecil didn't see her up ahead, it means she's turned off somewhere." Margaret looked up and down the road thoughtfully. "I wonder," she said softly. She rode about fifty yards back the way they'd come. Then she stopped.

A footpath joined the road there.

"I wonder," Margaret said, frowning.

"What makes you think she went there?" Stephen asked, perplexed.

Margaret didn't answer. She shook her head as if she was having trouble believing something.

Stephen, exasperated, walked a few paces up the path. And stopped dead.

On a patch of dirt at his feet was the faint, crescent-moon impression of someone's heel. Stephen bent down to examine it. The print looked fresh in the damp earth. A few feet beyond was a full footprint. It was a small foot in a small shoe. It looked exactly like the prints Stephen had seen only a short while ago at the stream.

He ran up the path.

In less than a hundred yards, he came to a small clearing. He halted at the edge and looked around. There was a small hut at the other side of the clearing. Smoke curled from a hole in the roof. The door stood open. Lucy's basket had been placed to one side. Stephen's heart pounded. He fully expected Howard Makepeese to step into the light and take flight. Stephen was sure he couldn't run fast enough to catch him. Makepeese might even elude James and Margaret in the woods. The list would be lost forever.

But no one came out of the hut.

Wind whispered in the branches, which clattered together, and stirred fallen leaves on the ground. The only other sounds were those of horses' hooves faint upon the path. Margaret and James dismounted and joined him at the edge of the clearing. No voices, no sounds of movement came from the hut, however. It was as if no one was there but the intruders.

Something was odd. Something about the scene was not right.

Stephen motioned for James and Margaret to remain where they were. He drew his dagger and crossed the clearing.

He paused at the door and glanced in the hut.

It was a small hut, with room for a hearth on the floor and a straw pallet of a bed, which lay in one corner.

But that was not all.

There were two naked people in the hut. A man and woman.

Both of them lay on their backs, the man beside the bed, the woman with her legs off its end.

Both of them had been stabbed numerous times.

Both were dead.

Stephen pushed the door all the way to the wall, half expecting someone to be hiding behind it. The door clunked against a metallic object, then clumped against the wall. He put his dagger away and stepped into the hut. Two piles of clothes lay by the door, one for the man and one for the woman. A belt with an empty dagger scabbard lay beside the piles of clothes.

Stephen knelt beside the bodies. What he had first taken for a woman looked on closer examination to be a girl of only fifteen or sixteen. She had been stabbed at least a dozen times in the upper chest and neck.

The man was Howard Makepeese. Even the indignity of death did not rob him of his youthful handsomeness. He had what looked like more than two dozen wounds to the chest. Stephen rolled Makepeese over. There were three wounds in his back. One of them seemed to have severed his spine. That was probably the one that killed him.

Silhouettes filled the door.

"Good God!" Margaret said.

Stephen looked up at her.

Margaret asked, "Is that him?"

"Yes."

"What . . . what happened?"

Stephen rose and walked into the light. He was glad to get out of that hut. Death seemed to permeate every cranny and left him feeling unclean. He said heavily, "I think Lucy's had her revenge."

"What do you mean?"

"The bodies are as warm as you and I. They've just been killed. I think Lucy found them here naked and lost control of herself." He gestured toward the empty scabbard. "She used Makepeese's own dagger." He thought of the metal object encountered by the door. He went inside to retrieve it and came out with a dagger that had blood on the blade all the way to the cross. "Here it is." He put the dagger on the ground by the door. "The question now is, where's she gone?"

"I know," James said. He was at a corner of the hut, pointing toward something to the rear.

Stephen and Margaret joined him there and received another shock.

Lucy was there, all right — hanging from a tree limb by a length of cloth torn from the hem of her skirt.

Chapter 17

Stephen held up Lucy's body while James clambered into the tree and slashed the rope. Lucy collapsed across Stephen's shoulder. He laid her on the ground and pried the loop of fabric from around her neck, where it had bitten deeply into the flesh. She was still as warm as life, as the others had been, and her eyelids fluttered. When the coil came off, her chest heaved as she tried to breathe, and by some miracle, her heart was still beating — Stephen could feel the pulse in her neck with his fingers.

But it was for nothing. She slipped away under his hands.

"Is s-she —?" Margaret stammered. Like anyone else she was accustomed to death, but three dead at once and so violently in such a peaceful place still was a shock.

"Yes," Stephen said. "We're too late."

"A pity," Margaret said. She wheeled about and marched back to the hut.

Stephen rose quickly to follow her.

He found Margaret paused at the doorway, hands on the sides. There was a stricken look on her face. He pulled her gently aside. "I'll look for it," he said. "No need for you to go in."

"Thank you," she said. "I thought I could bear it, but I cannot."

He rifled through the piles of clothes, pulled up the blanket from beneath the girl's body and shook it out, then brought the straw pallet out of the hut and into the light. There was nothing on the ground under it so if the pallet had been used to hide anything, it was inside. Like most such pallets it was a linen sack sewn shut at only one end; the other was left open and folded over so the stuffing could be replaced periodically. Stephen and Margaret upended the sack and dumped the contents on the ground. They found only straw.

"He doesn't have it," Stephen said at last, trying not to sound as crushed as he felt. He had been certain that when he found Howard Makepeese he would find the list.

"Perhaps it's still inside," Margaret said. "Perhaps he's hidden it somewhere."

Stephen went over every inch of the walls, but he found no niche or cranny that held hidden secrets, and there was no sign that anything had been buried under the floor. Stephen even kicked the smoldering fire aside and probed the ground underneath in case Makepeese had been so clever as to conceal the treasure there, where most people wouldn't think to look.

Margaret put her head on his chest when he had finished. "I'm sorry, Stephen. I'm so sorry."

"It's all right," he said, although it didn't feel all right. He was lost, without any idea what to do. There was always Muryet's lover, but he doubted that fellow knew anything useful.

"Might as well eat," James said. "Those poor bastards got no use for all this now." James, who had seated himself by the door, was exploring Lucy's basket. He pulled out a small ham, a large round of goat cheese, and two loaves of dark bread. There were also a couple of clay pots. One of them held bean paste and the other honey. "No butter. Too bad."

Stephen's galloping hunger reasserted itself at the sight of all that food and the old soldier in him would not allow the presence of death to interfere with a meal. Margaret hesitated, then after a moment, joined them.

"We can't leave them just to lie here," she said, spooning bean paste with the help of the only spoon in the basket. "My, this is good. Oil and mustard, I think."

Her voice seemed calm, but Stephen noticed her hands trembled ever so slightly. "I'll have to contact the local authority," Stephen said, "once I figure out who holds this land. He'll summon the hundred bailiff for this area who'll get a jury together. It will be a short inquest, though. A formality, really. But formalities must be observed."

Margaret was quiet, staring into the bean pot. Then she said, "I can help you with that."

"You can?"

"Yes. I know who holds this land. You've met him, in fact. This is Marlbrook land. That fellow you met on the road holds it — Cecil Marlbrook."

"Ah."

She went on, "There's a path behind the tree where we found . . . her . . . Lucy. At the fork bear right. It leads to the Marlbrook manor. His steward should be there. He'll help you." She stood suddenly, wiping her hands on her skirts. Her voice was agitated. "I must go. I can't stand it here. You'll forgive me if I don't accompany you. James!" she said and turned toward the horses, which were grazing on grass and weeds at the edges of the clearing, their mouths a sickly greenish white.

James lifted her to the back of her mare. He mounted the other and followed her down the path. Within moments, the soft thuds of the horses' hooves were swallowed by the forest and it was quiet.

Stephen hated to see her go. Even in such a distressing place, he felt drawn to her, and that attraction caused him to wander down the path after her, lost in fantasies about what might be between them but probably, he had to admit, never would.

He had gone about twenty yards before he came to his senses and turned back. The path curved sharply before it reached the hut, and Stephen cut across the center of the curve, which took him through a brief tongue of forest. He had taken only three steps off the path before he had to leap unexpectedly over a pile of horse dung. It was fresh dung, still moist and green and smelly with that unmistakable odor of horse manure. When he held his palms over it, he found that it was still warm. The animal that had left this pile had been here only minutes ago.

But neither his, Margaret's, nor James' horse had stood here. They had been tethered in the clearing.

Stephen stood up and scanned the forest but saw nothing human or horse concealed within the undergrowth or behind the bare trunks of the trees.

His discovery was disquieting and more than a little unnerving. He had no answer why a horse had been there without any of them being aware of it. His shadow, that boy, had not had a horse, and he doubted the lad could ride in any case. Perhaps it had been one of Marlbrook's foresters, pausing to see what they were about.

He reached the clearing, passed the hut, and paused at the head of the path Margaret had told him was there. It was an old path and not well worn; hardly more than a depression in the leaves of the forest floor, as faint and subtle as a game trail. He gazed around the clearing, with its tumble-down forester's hut and the corpse by the big tree, as if it might speak its secrets to him. But no sound came, not even the call of a bird, nor any illumination of the mind.

Leading the gelding, he turned and started down the path to Marlbrook.

Chapter 18

Stephen remained at Marlbrook for two days. It took until late Tuesday to assemble the hundred's jury and hold the inquest, with Stephen acting as his own clerk. And then, surprisingly, Cecil Marlbrook, despite his initial reserve, proved to be a congenial host and insisted that he stay overnight. Stephen allowed himself to be persuaded. Now that Howard Makepeese was dead, he had lost his last lead to the list. There was no point in rushing back to confess his failure to Valence, and it would be some time before Gilbert returned from his errand. And it was pleasant to lose himself in games and drink. It had been years since he had just lolled around an English manor as if he had nothing in the world to do.

By the time Stephen took his leave, it was late afternoon, the sun less than an hour off the western horizon, casting long mournful shadows through the bare trees. There had been so much drinking after dinner that Stephen had trouble climbing into the saddle, although he had the benefit of a mounting block to assist him so he didn't have to suffer the embarrassment of mounting on the right. He swayed a bit, which drew laughter from Marlbrook's male guests, but it was good humored and not malicious. They were young men Stephen's age or younger, most of them still without property, and because of that lack prone to the landless young gentryman's sense of irresponsibility. Of their group only Marlbrook had come into land, and that only a few years ago. There seemed to be a story behind his inheritance, but nobody was willing to talk about it. Two of the men found a child's ball they'd found lying in the yard and started a game of catch, then one of them impulsively threw the ball at Stephen, who ducked, nearly falling off his horse again, to an even greater outburst of laughter.

Marlbrook held the gelding's bridle to say his farewell. "I apologize for my loutish friend," he said. "I'll have him thrashed if you like."

"It's all right," Stephen said. "No danger there. He couldn't have hit himself with that ball if he'd held it over his head."

It was a poor joke, but everyone was so drunk that they thought it was funny.

"Please feel free to come again," Marlbrook said, releasing the bridle. "I'd like to hear more of Spain. Fascinating country."

"Indeed it is," Stephen said, suppressing a hiccup. "Beautiful place, filled with beautiful women of easy virtue!" That was a lie, but men loved to think there were countries where women were eager to throw themselves at them. In truth, there were no such places, but fact was always less comforting than illusion.

"Here, here!" Those who had cups raised them and drank again to easy Spanish women.

Stephen waved and rode out of the yard. Marlbrook manor sat off the road at the end of a long track that ran through the village fields. When he reached the road, he halted. He got off the gelding. He walked up and down trying to think. A thought had been bothering him for the last two days, like a burr under a saddle or a splinter in the hand. He wasn't sure what to make of it, but now that he was away from Marlbrook, he had to face it. He looked around, surveying the land. The ground was fairly flat here, good for farming, except parts were a bit marshy and wet. A section of the field had been plowed up for planting winter wheat. But the day was so far gone that the villagers had all gone home for supper. Their thatched houses, where smoke drifted from holes in the roofs, were visible a couple hundred yards to the north. About an equal distance away, the manor house stood before a backdrop of forest, which curved around to enclose the southern field. The road south entered the forest as if into a tunnel. Above the forest to the south loomed a large hill about half a mile away that was covered with trees. He had trouble seeing all these things clearly. He had to cover one eye with the palm of a hand so they came into focus. The air was growing noticeably colder. He breathed deeply. He wished he had a drink of water.

It was about eight miles by road from here to Ludlow. On the gelding it should take about an hour to get there if he pushed it, which meant he could make it by sundown. The thought of the effort and the pounding of that ride made him want to shudder. Ordinarily, he would not have minded, but the trot was a hard gait, and he didn't feel up to it. He felt more like lying down and going to sleep right there by the road. The shorter route was north through Marlbrook village to Burington and then down the Aston road. But instead, Stephen remounted and rode south. Another village lay there, a quarter mile away through the forest, although he couldn't remember its name. He took the track to the village.

By the time Stephen reached it, he had a raging thirst. Lying at the foot of the big hill he'd seen earlier, it was a collection of timber-and-wattle huts, surrounded by their yards and gardens, that straggled along the road. The well was by the road directly across from the manor house, which sat at the road junction, a tall rectangular stone building with a red tiled roof. Stephen dropped the bucket in the well and pulled it up by its rope, for there was no pulley. There was a leather cup attached to the bucket handle by a length of leather string, but he didn't bother with the cup. He tipped the bucket up and drank directly from it. When he was done, he sat on the well's wooden wall, wishing he didn't have to get back on the horse. But he was feeling slightly better. He didn't have to hold one hand over an eye to see now.

A blacksmith and his two apprentices came over, having just knocked off work. They were covered with black soot and grime.

"You done with that bucket, sir?" the blacksmith asked.

"It's all yours," Stephen said.

The blacksmith held a large cake of soap, and he and the boys took turns washing off in the bucket.

Stephen realized that they did this every evening. He thought distastefully of the drink he had just taken.

"What village is this?" Stephen asked.

"Not from around here, are you, sir?" the blacksmith asked.

"I'm from west and north. Don't get around here much."

"It's called Adforton, sir. The village and the manor."

"Adforton," Stephen said, rolling the word around in his mouth. "I know someone from around here, I think."

"And who would that be, sir?" the blacksmith said with polite interest, although he didn't really care.

"Margaret de Thottenham is her name."

The blacksmith smiled, warming slightly. "Ah, that would be Lady Margaret. She grew up in that house right over here." He pointed toward the tall stone house, where smoke dribbled from the chimneys that stuck up at each end. "Her brother holds the manor now." He added, "We miss her father, the old master. A right good lord, he was." He stood up abruptly as if he had said more than he should have, for the tone implied that the brother was not as congenial a master as the father had been, and it did not do to criticize the lord to strangers. "Well, give my regards to Lady Margaret when you see her. Shame about her husband being killed and all. My name's Richard, Richard Smith."

"I'll do that Master Smith."

"Good evening to you, then, sir." Smith strode off with the apprentices in tow.

"And to you," Stephen said to his back. He pushed over the bucket so the grimy water spilled onto the ground.

Belatedly, another question swam into his head. But the smith and his boys had turned into the yard of a house fronting the road and were going in the door even as he started after them, about to call out. He should have thought to ask the question before letting the smith get away. I am drunk, he thought disgustedly. I've a mind like porridge.

People in town would know the answer — Gilbert would know the answer. Gilbert would be back soon; perhaps even at this moment, he was sitting down to supper at the Broken Shield. The hope that he had returned was the main reason

Baynard's List

Stephen had insisted on leaving this afternoon, although that was not the reason he had given.

Stephen mounted the gelding. He swung the horse's head north and slouched toward Ludlow.

Chapter 19

Stephen was sober by the time he descended the slope from Ludford and plodded across the Teme bridge. The jolting of the ride and the bitter chill of the night had brought him back to earth and kept him awake. Sobriety had not brought good feeling, however. His head was pounding, and he wished he could find a warm place to lie down and go to sleep.

The houses along Lower Broad Street were dark and shuttered, their inhabitants having retired for the night. Not for them was there any late night carousing, as there often was at the castle. These were working people who had to be up before dawn to attend to business. It was quiet and peaceful, except for the howl of cats fighting in a distant yard, the avenue bathed in the silver light of a three-quarters moon.

There were lights from candles and oil lamps leaving a glow around the shutters at the Wobbly Kettle, however, even though it was more than an hour after sundown. Several cloaked figures emerged from the front door and hurried away with an air of furtiveness as he rode by. When Stephen glanced to the right across the street from the Kettle, the reason for furtiveness became apparent. A spare hooded figure stood on the stoop of the doorway to St. John's Hospital as if taking tally of the Kettle's guests. Stephen recognized the figure when he came up to it.

"Good evening, prior," Stephen said. "Lovely evening, but a bit cold to be outdoors."

Prior Simon grunted, as if he had not expected to be spoken to. The prior said flatly, "I am studying the stars."

Stephen wasn't sure whether to believe this. "Ah, what do they tell us this evening?"

"I am not an astrologer," the prior said. "I am a natural philosopher."

"Oh," Stephen said, a little nonplused. He didn't know anything about natural philosophy himself. It was as mysterious as astrology or alchemy as far as he was concerned.

His education had been limited to Latin, rhetoric, rudimentary arithmetic, music, and, later, a smattering of the law. "Well, carry on then. Don't let me interrupt you."

"I won't. Good evening, sir."

"Same to you."

The town gates were shut and barred, of course. Gip answered his kick to the gate by opening the little view port he used to examine those who came calling after hours. When he saw who it was, to Stephen's surprise, Gip opened the sally port without giving him any trouble. Stephen ducked down and rode through.

"Heard about that terrible business with young Lucy," Gip said. "Is it true you found her hanging from a tree?"

"Yes," Stephen said.

"And she'd killed Howard Makepeese and that girl?"

"Dead as salted pork," Stephen said.

"Damn," Gip said. He shook his head. "I've heard of people going wild with jealousy, but it's usually a fellow, not a woman, causes the trouble."

"Yeah," Stephen said. He didn't want to talk about it. He just wanted to get home, see Gilbert, and fall into bed.

He twitched a rein and squeezed with his legs to tell the horse to continue up Broad Street. He was some distance up the street when he heard Gip say distinctly — how voices carry in the stillness and dark! — "He's back. Up you go. Just like I promised."

A youthful voice snarled, "Don't you kick me, you bastard!"

There was a thump and a sharp curse from Gip.

Stephen turned to see what this was about and caught sight of a small shadow slink from the gatehouse and merge with the greater shadow of one of the houses on the east side of the street.

His follower had caught up with him again. Stephen smiled thinly, although there was nothing humorous in the situation. You had to admire the boy's persistence.

Stephen scanned the street for other, larger and more dangerous shadows, but didn't see anything out of the ordinary, except for a pair of dogs trotting soundlessly up the street ahead. He looked back again, but couldn't see the boy. He thought momentarily about turning back to try to catch him. But he dismissed the idea. He was too tired and too slow to bag the boy, who'd just scamper down an alley and leap a fence far more quickly than he could.

Stephen hesitated at Bell Lane, which lay in shadow, a maw that could conceal attackers who might appear from nowhere and drag him from his horse before he had a chance to react. He didn't relish going down there, all of a sudden. He asked the gelding for a canter, and despite its fatigue, it obeyed, and before he knew it, he was at the Broken Shield's gate. It was barred from the inside as it always was at night, and he climbed over the fence by standing on the horse's back. Once inside, it was an easy matter to lift the bar, open the gate, and lead the horse inside, although he suffered some anxiety as he imagined a rush of feet coming at him before he got the gate shut and barred again.

He felt safe now, in the familiarity of the yard, which was awash in brilliant moonlight. The only odd thing was a large black cat he had never seen before, which sat unmoving in a spot of moonlight in the middle of the yard. Its head swivelled to follow his progress to the stable. Its eyes glowed eerily and there was something accusatory in their gleam, and he thought unaccountably of Lucy, as if her soul had somehow come back as the cat and was trying to tell him something.

Groping about in the pitch dark, he found an empty stall for the gelding. He removed the horse's tack and fumbled about for the grain bin, where he filled a bucket with oats. The gelding was so hungry that he nearly knocked the bucket out of Stephen's hands going for the oats.

After closing the gate, Stephen went left, running his hand along the wall, counting the stalls to locate Harry's. The black cat had come to the doorway and watched him pass. Stephen found its presence disturbing.

"Harry," Stephen called, "are you awake?"

"A dead man couldn't sleep through that racket," Harry grumbled. "What do you want?"

"Do you believe in ghosts?"

"Damn it, man, you didn't wake me up to ask that question, did you?"

"No."

"Well, then, get on with it. You're disturbing my rest."

Stephen glanced at the cat, which was licking a paw. "There's a boy about twelve, thin, brown hair that sticks out like a hay rick, looks like one of the urchins. I wondered if you knew him."

Harry grunted. "There's a dozen boys like that in town."

"He carries a knife and knows how to use it. I think you might have seen him hanging around Broad Gate."

There was a rustling as Harry sat up. "Yeah, there was a boy like that hanging around Broad Gate the last few days. Not doing much of anything, just sitting there across the way. Why?"

"He's been following me. He was waiting for me at Broad Gate when I rode in tonight."

"You don't say. What the hell for?"

Stephen told him quickly about his other encounters with the boy, how he'd been at the mouth of Bell Lane on the night he was attacked. "Do you know him?"

"Yeah. He's Will Thumper's son, Tad."

"Will Thumper," Stephen mused. He didn't know the name.

"You haven't heard of Thumper? That's not his real name, it's just what people call him, on account of he's a fighter and beats lots of people up — a big man and quick tempered. Favors a stave to his fists, though. Not bad with a knife, either. Word is, he makes his living as a thief, though no one's ever caught him at it. You don't think Thumper was in on that business the other night, do you?"

Favored staves, did he? Both of the men who'd attacked him Saturday night had used clubs. Stephen said: "I believe he was."

"Why would he take after you?"

"Because someone paid him to do it."

"Right. That makes sense. We all know that Nigel FitzSimmons wants you dead."

"Well, actually we don't know that."

"Who else could it have been?"

"I suppose to be certain I'll have to ask Thumper himself."

"As if he'd tell you," Harry snorted.

"Where does he live?"

"You're not really thinking about strolling over and asking him, are you?"

"Uh, yes. What else can I do? Where do I find him?"

"Huh. He's got a house in lower Galdeford, just beyond the Augustine friary. There's a brood of Thumpers there, more than a dozen of all ages and every one of them mean as a dog. I wouldn't go there alone if I was you."

"Harry, you're a prize."

"Ought to be worth something, it should."

"When Sir Geoff sends my wages, there'll be a little something for you."

Harry snorted. "Expect me to extend credit, do you? After Thumper kills you, no one will remember your debt."

"Good night, Harry."

Stephen withdrew to the yard and crossed to the inn. The black cat was sitting by the stoop and slunk away at his approach.

He hadn't noticed it at the front when he first arrived, but there was a candle or two burning in the hall of the inn. He could see the faint glow through a crack in the door. He tried the door and found it barred. But after a moment or two, the bar was lifted and the door opened to reveal Gilbert.

"Well, well," Gilbert said, stepping back to admit Stephen. "I wondered where you had got to. I thought I heard someone shutting the gate, but no one rang the bell, so I thought it had to be you." There was a bell by the door that late arrivals used to request admittance.

"How did it go?" Stephen asked.

"Ah, the boy," Gilbert said, closing the door. He crossed to a table by the fire, where Edith and Jennifer were sitting across from a place setting obviously meant for Gilbert's late supper. "Not to worry. He's safe. Your cousin was most congenial and very willingly took him in. Here, he sent you this letter. I have it here somewhere. Good Lord, I couldn't have lost it!" He rummaged through his large leather belt pouch and came out with a crushed sheet of vellum.

"I wasn't sure you'd be back by now. It's a long way into Powys."

"The roads were good, the weather was fine. We reached the manor the very first evening."

Stephen was surprised. "It's more than fifty miles away!"

Gilbert, who had returned to sit before his supper, slapped his thigh. "You couldn't have done as well — and with a child in my arms, too! You must promise never to make fun of my horsemanship again."

"No, I suppose I can't." Stephen smiled.

Gilbert wagged a finger. "I have witnesses. I'll hold you to that promise."

Stephen broke the green wax seal and unrolled the letter, thinking of the man who had written it. About eighty years ago, his great-grandmother's brother had married a Welsh woman and thereby acquired a manor in Powys. That branch of family was more Welsh than English now, although nominally they still supported the English king. He had met the current holder of the manor, who was really only a very distant cousin, when they were both boys at St. Laurence's school, and even then they were only together half a year.

It was a brief letter and did not take long to read it. Stephen looked up in astonishment when he was done. "He sent the mare back."

Gilbert smiled. "He said he did not need encouragement to aid a member of the family in distress."

"I am ashamed to have thought he might."

"He bids you come and stay with him, too, when you have done what you need to do here." Gilbert went on more briskly. "So, tell me what you've been up to these last few days." Gilbert eyed him narrowly as if he already knew.

Stephen told him briefly about following Lucy to Marlbrook and what he'd found when he got there.

Gilbert shook his head sadly. "A terrible, terrible business." He looked at Stephen closely. "You're sure this happened on Marlbrook land?"

"Yes. The lord made no bones about the fact it was his property."

Gilbert sucked his front teeth in thought. "It's an odd coincidence, you know."

"What is?"

"It hasn't struck you?"

"What's supposed to have struck me?"

"The irony of it. The strangeness."

"I'm not sure what you mean."

He spoke as if he was stating an obvious fact that Stephen should already know. "Olivia Baynard was born there. Makepeese and Lucy died on what used to be her family's land — before they lost it four years ago. Terrible thing, that, terrible stupid thing."

Stephen stared at the floor. His head felt full of sludge. This was the answer to the question he should have asked in Adforton. There was something important attached this answer, and it took some time to work its way through the sludge in his head. He wished again that he hadn't had so much to drink this afternoon.

"Clement," Stephen said, standing up. "Clement will know this."

"I'm sure he would," Gilbert said mildly. "Doubtless by now he's found out. The whole town knows about Lucy and

Makepeese. Bad news always travels faster than good. Especially that kind."

Stephen started toward the front door. "Then I must hurry. Olivia is in danger."

Chapter 20

"Olivia Baynard — in danger from Clement? How could that be possible?" Gilbert sputtered the question as he raced after Stephen when they emerged into Bell Lane. He could hardly keep pace with Stephen when the taller and younger man was walking, and now he was running.

"Howard Makepeese went to ground on Marlbrook land," Stephen said as they hurried toward Broad Street. "The fact he hid there means she hid him, which means she knows about the list. Clement may have the brains of a toad, but he isn't so stupid that he can't figure that much out."

A flicker of movement caught his eye at the mouth of the alley between Mistress Bartelott's house and the shoemaker's: it had to be a startled Tad Thumper scurrying out of sight.

"You've been out of touch, Master Gilbert!" Stephen said over his shoulder.

"Of course I've been out of touch! You sent me to Wales! Tell me what I've missed!"

"I haven't the time! I'll have to tell you when we get there!" Stephen turned the corner onto Broad Street and started up the hill. The street was bathed in moonlight, each rock and rut sharply outlined as if drawn on canvas with charcoal.

Gilbert found it harder going on the slope than on Bell Lane's relative flatness. He immediately fell farther and farther behind. His gasping receded as the distance between them grew. "Dear God, man, how do you expect me to be of any assistance when you keep me in the dark?"

When Stephen reached High Street, he encountered a pair of silhouetted figures in the middle of the street walking without a lantern in the direction of the castle — a man with his arm around a woman. They scuttled off at his approach, not wanting to be noticed. For they, like Stephen, were out after curfew.

He plunged into College Lane, which was in shadow due to the angle of the moon. In moments he was at the Baynard

House door. He pounded on it with his fist, gasping to catch his breath. Gilbert finally came up behind him and opened his mouth to ask a question, but Stephen ignored him and continued pounding.

After a long wait, the door cracked open. The white blob of a face peered through the crack. It was one of the young grooms, a boy barely old enough to shave.

"Who is it?" a man's hard voice asked behind him.

The boy peered at Stephen as if he was having trouble telling who it was in the dark.

"It's Stephen Attebrook," Stephen said to make things easier for him.

"What do you want?" the invisible man asked in a hostile voice.

Stephen recognized the voice. It belonged to Margaret's retainer, James. He overlooked the man's lack of respect and said, "I've come to see Olivia Baynard."

"She isn't here."

"What do you mean, she isn't here?"

"Just what I said. She's gone."

There was the sound of scraping feet on the tiled floor inside and the low hasty mutter of voices.

Then the door swung fully open.

Holding a candle, Margaret stood there with James and Walter beside her in positions that looked very protective. Stephen noticed that each man held a dagger barely concealed from view by his thigh.

Margaret wore a nightdress with a cloak thrown over her shoulders but not drawn together enough to conceal the delicious points of her nipples beneath the thin fabric of the nightdress. Her long blonde hair was undone and cascaded in ringlets over her shoulders. She was indescribably beautiful in the golden light of the candle.

She said, "Olivia isn't here, Stephen."

"Where did she go?"

"I don't know. She was gone when I returned. No one knows what's happened to her. It's as though she's vanished from the face of the earth."

"She was invited for dinner at the castle Monday," Margaret said. "She went out and never came back."

Stephen stopped in front of the fire, which flared from the wood shavings the boy had thrown on the banked coals to restart the blaze. "And no one's seen her?"

"We asked, Stephen," Margaret said. "She didn't reach the castle. She walked out the front door of the house and disappeared."

"You're sure she isn't there after all?"

"Where?"

"The castle. It has to be Clement's doing." Briefly he told her about the pile of dung he had found. "We followers were ourselves followed, it seems. It had to be him or one of his people. He, more than anyone else, would understand the significance of Howard Makepeese hiding at Marlbrook."

"What significance is there to that?" Gilbert asked, bewildered.

Margaret looked grim and answered Stephen instead of Gilbert. "And he beat me back to Ludlow."

"With enough time to spare to snatch Olivia," Stephen said.

Margaret put her face in her hands. "Oh, God forgive me for stopping for a drink."

"How can it be Clement's doing — if you pardon my asking," Gilbert said.

Neither Margaret nor Stephen satisfied him now. Margaret looked up and said to Stephen, "I thought she might be at the castle. So I sent Walter to enquire if she was there, but she's not. I trust Walter to be sure."

"Damn," Stephen said.

"What is going on?" Gilbert burst out.

"Clement is after the list in competition with Stephen," Margaret said at last tiring of his interruptions. "The fact Makepeese was hiding at Marlbrook has to mean that she sent him there." As she spoke, her eyes met Stephen's. He nodded. She went on, "If she sent him there, she must be involved in the disappearance of the list and may know something about its whereabouts. Clement must understand this, so she is in terrible danger. Clement has convinced Valence to give him the power to arrest and question people. An unfair advantage, I'm afraid, and they will not be tender when they use it."

"Oh, my," Gilbert said. "No one is safe."

"Quite so," Margaret said with bitterness. "One is never safe from men with unchecked power. You can be sure they will abuse it."

Stephen stopped pacing. "I think I know one place to look for her."

Chapter 21

Stephen stepped out into the cold October night. He shut the door loudly behind him. He spat on the street. He scratched himself. He looked up and down College Lane. It was quiet and dark. He saw no one. Nor did he expect to. Not yet anyway.

He turned north toward Linney Gate at the end of the lane. It was a sally port, wide enough to admit only a man on horseback. Like the other gates through the town wall, it was barred for the night. But since this was a time of peace and to save money, there was no warden to guard it. Stephen lifted the bar, opened the door, and slipped through to the other side.

No bridge spanned the town ditch here because the gate was not supposed to be used except in emergencies, although a footpath dipped across the ditch and led downhill through a moon-washed field. Stephen closed the gate and pressed himself against the wall to one side and waited.

Presently, the gate door opened a crack. There was a pause, as though whoever had cracked it was looking out to see if the coast was clear. Then it swung a bit farther. Stephen sensed rather than saw the small thin figure that slipped through the opening.

Stephen grabbed a handful of collar, intending to sweep the boy's feet from beneath him. But the boy avoided the sweep, kicked Stephen painfully in the leg, and raked Stephen's hands away from his collar.

Then he ducked back through the door to escape.

Stephen rubbed his injured shin, embarrassed that the boy had got away.

The gate opened again, but this time there was no stealth in it. Gilbert stood in the gap. "The little tripe proved to be a bit too much for you, eh?" he said.

"Shut up," Stephen said. His pride was too wounded for any other reply.

Gilbert stepped aside and Stephen could see the dark figures of James and Walter, who held Tad Thumper between them.

"Careful," Stephen said. "It's Will Thumper's boy. He carries a knife and knows how to use it."

"We found it," James said. He handed the knife to Stephen, who stuck it in his belt.

Stephen leaned down to Tad's level. Even in partial shadow, the boy's face was knotted with defiance. "You know, Tad," Stephen said softly, "these men are not gentle. If you don't answer my questions honestly, they may become angry. They are not my men. They belong to Lady Olivia's good friend, who worries about her welfare. I have no control over what they might do."

Tad spat and told Stephen to place one body part into another.

"Your father has done a terrible thing, Tad," Stephen said calmly. "I know he did it because Clement asked him to, but in this thing Clement is not acting for Valence. His lordship will be very angry when he finds out. Clement will not be able to protect him his time. Or you, or your family."

Tad cursed him again, but his manner was a little less vigorous than before.

"But she has a good friend, who will take up her cause," Stephen said. "And if the lady is not redeemed, your family will be killed — if not all at once, then one after another. Since we have you, I am afraid we will have to hand you over to James and Walter, here."

The boy's lips tightened, but he said nothing.

"But if you tell us what we need to know," Stephen went on, "no harm will befall you or anyone."

Tad was quiet for a moment. "You won't hurt anyone?"

"I don't want anyone to be hurt, if it can be avoided. We just want the lady back."

Tad was quiet again. Then he said, "All right."

"Is she at your dad's house?" The Thumper house in Lower Galdeford, beyond the priory, Harry had said.

"Yes."

"How is she?"

"I don't know. She's kept in one of the back rooms. I never see her."

"But she's alive."

"Was this afternoon when I went to supper. I could hear her crying for a time before —" he broke off.

"Before what?"

"Before dad beat her some to make her shut up."

"Well, at least she's still alive," Stephen said more to the men than to the boy.

Tad grunted. "That won't last long. Clement said that tomorrow we're supposed to take her out in the countryside and . . ." He hissed and jerked his head.

Stephen's gut curled. Clement meant to have Olivia's throat cut. If they didn't free her tonight, she'd die tomorrow. "Show me the layout of your house," he said. He knelt down and gestured to Walter to release one of Tad's arms.

The boy traced the outlines of a roughly U-shaped structure with a finger in a patch of road illuminated by a spot of moonlight. At Stephen's prompting, he indicated one of the wings as the storeroom where Olivia was a prisoner.

"Thank you, Tad," Stephen said, standing up. "If you're lying about this, though, you know I can't protect you. It's a hard world, and I'm sorry."

"You won't let dad know I told you?" Tad asked, suddenly anxious.

"Certainly not."

"What do we do with him?" James asked.

"Take him back to the house," Stephen said. "Better tie him up and have one of the grooms sit with him. He's as slippery as an eel. It's the only way we'll be able to hold him."

"Yessir," James said.

They retreated into the gloom of College Lane, while Stephen and Gilbert waited at the gate.

When James and Walter returned, Margaret was with them, muffled in a voluminous cloak against the cold so that not even her face was visible.

"Margaret," Stephen said worriedly, "this is no place for a woman. There could be fighting."

"They told me what's happened. Olivia will need aid and comfort you'll not be able to provide her," Margaret said stiffly. "Besides, I can use a knife as well as any man." She gave a short laugh and added, "Ask James. He taught me how."

James grinned ruefully and nodded.

"Good," Margaret said. "Let's be off. Time is wasting."

"And we're going – where?" Gilbert wheezed as Stephen led them into the town ditch.

"Thumper's house."

"Ah, of course. I should have known."

Under the wooden bridge at Corve Street, they surprised three sleeping figures huddled by the remains of a fire: beggars or travelers who could not afford accommodations. The sleepers sat up in alarm at the group's approach, but Stephen spoke to them in warning. "Stay where you are. We're passing through and mean you no harm."

Even so, the beggars scrambled out of the way and stood to one side, watching the group pass beneath the bridge.

The ditch turned sharply to the right, following the town wall, and in less than a hundred yards they were at Galdeford Road, which announced its presence by another wooden bridge over the ditch.

Stephen climbed out of the ditch to the road and took the right fork, which led southeast. As he passed the stone cross at the fork, he saw an owl sitting on one if its limbs. The owl raised its wings and hooted. Stephen brought a finger to his lips and shushed it. The owl regarded them gravely and did not fly away. Stephen was glad to see the owl. Owls always meant good luck.

After a hundred yards, the lines of houses on either side of the road ended abruptly. On the left was an open pasture, on the right an apple orchard.

Gilbert tapped Stephen's shoulder. Stephen stopped to see what he wanted. Gilbert gestured at the orchard.

"You might want to go that way," Gilbert said. "The back door is often better for this kind of work than the front."

"Do you know the way?" Stephen asked.

"I wandered in that field a few times in my youth."

Stephen grinned. "Stealing apples or chasing girls?"

Gilbert harrumphed and pretended to be offended. "Neither, my boy. Seeking spiritual guidance alone in the wilderness."

"Let's not waste any more time," Margaret said behind them.

"Yes, my lady," Gilbert said hastily.

Gilbert clambered with some difficulty over the wattle fence separating the orchard from the road. The others followed with considerable more agility, including Margaret, who proved she could leap a fence as well as any man even when encumbered by skirts.

Gilbert then led them single file through the grove, weaving among the trees, blobs of moon shadow beneath each one, stumbling occasionally on late-ripening apples the harvesters had not found in the tall grass.

Buildings loomed to the left. One of them looked like the tower to a church. As they crept on and the view changed, Stephen could see it was unfinished. Scaffolding clung to one side and there was a notch in one edge of the top where the stonework was not complete.

Presently they came to another wattle fence. A manure pile lay just beyond it, a gray hump in the bright moonlight. The pile and a shed beside it shielded them from view from the house.

"You're sure this is it?" Stephen whispered.

"Quite sure," Gilbert said confidently.

They hopped this fence, too.

"Are there dogs?" Stephen asked as they reached the edge of the manure pile and the house came into full view. It was a rambling, squat, timbered house beneath its tall cap. It looked as though it had been added onto several times, and some if it was so old that it seemed about to crumble before their eyes.

"How should I know that?" Gilbert asked. "We'll soon find out if there are, won't we."

Stephen imagined a big mastiff bursting out of a shadow to fasten on his leg. He hefted the club James had given him at the town gate, wishing he had a sword instead. "I'll go. The rest of you wait here."

He was half way across the yard to the house before he realized that none of them had obeyed him. They'd only hesitated so that he got some distance ahead, then followed. He had a pang of anger at being disobeyed, but then, his little band wasn't an army and couldn't be expected to obey like one.

He reached the house and crouched beneath one of the rear windows on the wing Tad had indicated in his map. The window was shuttered of course against the night.

Gilbert knelt beside him. "Now what?" he whispered almost soundlessly. "Can't exactly knock on the door now, can we?"

Stephen brought his finger to his lips in alarm, fearful that even that tiny sound could be heard indoors. The truth was, he hadn't really thought out what to do once they had arrived. He hoped that the others besides Gilbert hadn't guessed that yet.

Stephen stood up and examined the window. Right away, he noticed something odd about it. Normally shutters opened outward. He had been expecting this and had thought he might pull the trick he had learned for opening hinged devices: forcing out the pins in the hinge and just removing the shutter. But since the shutters opened inward all the hinges were on the inside of the house. It was almost as if whoever had hung the shutters had anticipated that thieves might try to gain access that way.

He'd have to find another way in.

He ran his fingers along the plaster between the timbers that formed the frame of the house. An exploratory tap told him the plaster was unusually thick and solid. He'd need an ax to break through the plaster and wattle between the timbers and even if he had an ax, it would make enough noise to wake the inhabitants.

"Lift me to the roof," Stephen whispered to James and Walter.

They looked at him as if he had lost his mind. A plan came to him then, and Stephen whispered quickly into James ear. James looked doubtful, then smiled and nodded. The two grooms each took a leg and lifted Stephen up so he could grasp a handful of thatch. He hung on, worried about sliding off because the roof was so steep.

Roofing thatch is nothing more than thick bundles of straw tied together and lashed to slat supports. Sometimes it was thick enough and strong enough that a man could stand on it without falling through. But often the bundling was not so thick, and it was not uncommon, when people ventured onto roofs, that they fell through to the rooms below. Stephen took out his dagger and began to dig through the bundles beneath him, hoping this was a thin roof but also concerned that it might give way, as had happened the last time he had tried climbing onto a thatched roof.

The cracking of the thatch made a lot of noise in the quiet of the night. Stephen cringed at the racket, but he was too committed now to slow down or stop.

Within a few moments, he'd dug a hole by cutting the cords holding the bundles together which was broad enough to slip through. Although he now had his entryway, he did not go through yet. He looked for James, who was trotting across from the shed by the manure pile.

James waved and nodded. Then he led the others into hiding on the north side of the house.

There was nothing to do but wait and hold on.

An orange glow began to emanate from the shed. It quickly grew in size and intensity as the dry hay within the shed began to burn.

Presently, shouts of alarm were heard from within the house. There were thuds and clamoring. A boy, then a grown man emerged from the back door and ran to the shed.

Stephen swung his legs into the dark hole in the roof before they had a chance to notice him and dangled for a moment. He could not see what lay below, but it was too late to do anything about that. His course had been decided as soon as he had climbed to the roof. He let himself drop.

One foot landed on a barrel, another on a wicker basket. The barrel was too unsteady to hold him and the wicker basket collapsed. Stephen fell heavily on his side with a great thump, the wind knocked out of him. At least the floor's dirt, he thought, glad he hadn't broken a leg or twisted an ankle.

He sat up, listening for the sounds of alarm and nursing his bad foot, which ached from the fall. But although he heard considerable commotion, none of it seemed to be aimed at his entrance.

Despite the sealed shutters, light from the growing fire and the moon leaked through to provide some illumination, and Stephen was able to see that seemed to be a storeroom, filled with boxes and barrels and baskets and furniture all thrown together every which way, as if someone had just tossed it in the room without any thought to organization. He fumbled through and over the mess to one of the windows on the north side of the house, unlatched a shutter, and swung it open.

The faces of James, Walter, and Gilbert appeared immediately.

"We have to hurry, while they're occupied," Stephen said.

"I can't believe you've done this!" Gilbert said. "An arsonist! You've made me an arsonist!"

"Can't be helped, old man. James! Walter, come! Gilbert and Margaret, you wait here. Keep out of sight. Pretend you're a stone or something."

"I can't believe I let myself get involved in this!" Gilbert said. "I'm a law abiding man! This is madness! Arson! They hang people for arson!"

"Get down and keep quiet, you old fool," Margaret hissed as James and Walter clambered through the window.

Stephen led them across the room to the door, which was plainly visible now that a window was open. He crouched at the door and listened.

He eased up the latch and put an eye to the crack.

It was dark in this room, too dark to see anything other than the faintly illuminated outlines of another door some distance away.

Stephen pushed the door open and began creeping across the room on his hands and knees so as not to bump into anything and make unnecessary noise.

He had gone about ten feet when the door opened and a young woman carrying an oil lamp entered the room. She didn't notice him at first. When she did, she opened her mouth to scream.

Stephen was on his feet and had her by the throat to stifle the shout of alarm before she could call out.

"If you make a sound, it will be your last," he said.

The woman's eyes were wide with fear. She nodded.

Stephen motioned for Walter or James to close the door. He passed the woman, who was broad-waisted with pregancy, to Walter. "Bind and gag her," he said.

Stephen took the oil lamp and only then did he see what had brought the woman into the room.

A woman was sitting with her back to a post behind him. A rope was tied around her neck and leashed her to the post. She was covered by a filthy wool blanket. Her hair was a disheveled corona and her face was badly bruised. One eye was swollen shut, her nose was broken, and there was blood on her face and chin. A disgusting looking rag had been used as a gag. Stephen had never seen a person look so miserable.

Stephen knelt beside her so filled with sudden fury that he could hardly speak. The knot of the gag had been tied so tightly that he couldn't untie it. He had to cut the gag with his dagger. He also cut the rope leash.

The woman's head sagged and she began to cry.

"I'm so sorry, Olivia," Stephen said.

There wasn't time to talk about what had happened. Stephen grasped her by the shoulders and lifted her to her feet.

And got a second shock — for the blanket fell away and revealed that she was naked, her alabaster skin covered with bruises.

Olivia cried harder at her embarrassment, although she had the sense to stifle the sound. She couldn't even use her hands to conceal herself, because they were bound behind her.

Stephen cut those bonds, too, and threw his cloak over her. It was the best he could do.

The door to the front of the house opened again. A man rushed in, snarling, "Letti what the devil are you —"

The words caught in his throat when he saw the tableau before him: Stephen standing protectively with Olivia, Walter binding the woman.

Then James clouted him on the head. He stumbled, opened his mouth to shout, and Stephen had him by the throat, and stepping behind him, threw him hard to the ground.

Stephen pressed his dagger blade to the man's cheek. "If you make a sound," Stephen snarled, "I'll cut your face off."

The impulse to kill the man was almost overpowering, but Stephen resisted it with great effort, although he could not resist pounding the man above the ear with the pommel of his dagger before flipping him on his stomach.

Stephen tied the man's hands while James gagged him with the same disgusting rag they had used on Olivia.

Then Stephen tied the door latch. It would slow, but not stop, people from entering the room and buy them some time if anyone else came to investigate.

Stephen went ahead into the back storeroom with the oil lamp. James and Walter carried Olivia, who could not walk. James and Walter passed Olivia out the window to Gilbert and Margaret, while Stephen stood guard. Then they slipped through the window. Stephen blew out the lamp and followed.

The yard around the house was filled with furious activity. Neighbors had turned out to fight the fire, as they always did in such emergencies. Someone had organized a bucket brigade. There weren't enough people to pass the buckets hand-to-hand from the well across the road. Instead, people rushed by carrying buckets, in their hurry sloshing a good portion of their contents on the ground. So far, it did not seem that anyone had paid them any particular attention. They were just part of the crowd, and Stephen hoped it would stay that way, even though it must look a little odd to be carrying a woman wrapped in a cloak cross the yard to the fence.

They were almost to the fence and relative safety when a gravelly voice called out, "Hey! You!" Then, "Will! She's loose! She's getting away!"

There was no doubt who he meant.

The little rescue party began to run.

Gilbert vaulted the fence with agility he had not displayed before. Margaret leaped the fence as if it was not there. They turned to take Olivia, but James and Walter had stumbled and dropped her short of the fence. Stephen, right behind them, scooped her up, shouting at them to go, and they dashed and leaped and turned arms out. Stephen lurched to the fence and tossed Olivia, surprised at his own strength, for she literally flew through the air, losing the protection of the cloak, her legs and arms flailing, and would have crashed to the ground if Walter had not caught her in his arms.

Stephen was about the vault the fence himself. Then James shouted a warning.

Stephen ducked to one side. A club crashed into the fence where he had been only an instant before. There was a blur and he danced back, and another club swished an inch in front of his face, audibly humming in the air. He remembered his own club, which he'd put in his belt at the small of his back when he climbed to the roof.

He drew out his own stave as the first man at him pulled back for a second blow. The attacker put all his weight into it, his face a rictus at the effort. Stephen slipped slightly to the right as the blow fell and raised his own staff to the hanging point so that the blow ran off his weapon as water does a roof. Without pause, Stephen whipped his point around and struck the man on the top of his head. The blow sounded like he had knocked on a door instead of a man's skull, and the impact jarred Stephen's arm to his shoulder. Had the blow been from a sword, the man's head would have been parted to his collar bone, but as it was, the fellow merely blinked as if surprised by something.

Stephen was as surprised as his enemy, but more for the lack of effect of his blow than the damage it had done. He hesitated what might have been a fatal moment, which allowed a second man to close and aim another massive blow at his head that seemed to come all the way from the dung pile in the distance.

He ducked beneath this attack and struck the fellow in the short ribs with his left fist. It was like punching a post, but the man grunted at the impact, giving Stephen some satisfaction. He did not linger to savor it, but rammed the point of his staff under the man's chin and the second attacker toppled backward.

Stephen did not pause this time to relish the fellow's landing. He turned and vaulted the fence before any of the others had a chance at him.

It seemed as though the fence would hardly slow the other two down. But then they hesitated, as James arrived at Stephen's elbow to even the odds, for it was really now two against two, as the man Stephen has struck on the head sat down while a stream of blood ran down his face and dripped from his nose.

"Check, Will," Stephen said, directing this to a short muscular fellow with graying black hair. Stephen recognized him as one of the attackers in Bell Lane.

"What?" Will asked.

"Never mind. Figure of speech, not that you have much use for that sort of thing."

"I have use enough when it suits me."

"All right, then. Let's talk with words rather than staves. I've got Mistress Baynard back. Found her in your house. Odd thing that."

"Don't know what you're talking about."

"You've a short memory. Clement put you up to it?"

"Don't know a Clement."

"I've known liars in my time, but you're one of the worst. If you don't talk fast, you're going to have to answer to Valence why you and Clement had Lady Olivia prisoner in your house and why she was so abused. And then there's your storeroom. I don't think you're going to want the shire bailiffs rummaging through there. You'll have to explain where it all came from."

Thumper's face twitched. It was as though he had suddenly realized what tonight's events could cost him, which was plenty, since the goods in the storeroom were undoubtedly stolen.

Stephen said gently, "If you tell me what I want to know, I'll forget what I've seen and we'll call it even."

"What about the lady?"

"I think she'll be satisfied if Clement alone pays for what's happened."

"He's got powerful friends. You don't know."

Stephen suddenly became aware that everyone who had come to fight the fire had stopped to watch the fight. Beyond, the shed was a forgotten ruin, the sides and roof fallen in, flames leaping up like an All Hallow's Eve bonfire. He leaned close now so that only Thumper could hear and snarled, "I don't want your testimony. I just want to know. It was Clement, wasn't it."

Thumper licked his lips. "Yes," he said at last.

"Behind all of it — that business at Bell Lane the other night, Mistress Baynard's kidnapping."

Thumper nodded.

"Why did he kidnap Mistress Baynard?"

"He thought she knew where some letters was."

"Did she know?"

"She said she had them at Helen Webbere's but they was lost." Thumper looked apologetic: "He pressed her pretty hard. If she knew anything more, she'd have said so."

"She . . . you say she took it to Webbere's?"

"Aye. Was going to sell them."

"To whom?"

"Look, I don't know the whole of it. Clement did the asking himself and wouldn't let us listen. Only way I know is I had my ear to the door a little. I can't tell you more than that."

Stephen couldn't tell how much Thumper was holding back. But he had to trust that what he'd heard was true. He said, "You and I will forget about what's happened between us. If that's not satisfactory to you, we'll continue this discussion with steel — at a time and place of my choosing."

Thumper paused a moment, his eyes flicking to the unconscious men lying on the ground. He nodded.

"Good night, Will. My apologies about the mess."

Chapter 22

Stephen put his stick in his belt. His bad foot ached badly and he wished he could sit down. He was so tired all of a sudden. But there still was a lot to do yet.

James fell in beside him as Stephen strode through the orchard in the direction of Lower Galdeford Road. "Are you all right, sir?" he asked in a respectful tone that he had never used before.

"I seem to be in one piece," Stephen said. "Where are the others?"

"Gone on ahead, sir. I held back to see if you needed help, but things happened so fast I'm afraid I was useless to you."

"Things have a habit of happening fast. But I appreciate it."

They caught up with Margaret and the others as they were passing the unfinished church.

"That's the Augustine priory, isn't it," Stephen said to Gilbert, who was helping to carry Olivia.

"It is," Gilbert gasped.

"I thought I saw a couple of friars among the crowd who'd come to fight the fire," Stephen said.

"Do you mind if someone takes over for me?" Gilbert panted. "I'm nearly at the end of my rope. I'm sorry, my lady, but you seem to have gained twelve stone in just the time it's taken to come this far."

James took Gilbert's place. Shortly they reached the crossroad before Galdeford Gate. They descended to the ditch and went round the town the way they had come. Linney Gate was not barred or latched when they reached it, as though the watch never ventured down College Lane to check it during rounds. Margaret went ahead, followed by Walter and James carrying Olivia, then Gilbert. Stephen paused at the gate while the others hurried the few steps to the front door of Baynard House. He nodded to himself, drew the gate shut, but did not slide the bar into place.

When Stephen reached the hall, he found Gilbert sunk into a chair. The boy Tad was sitting in another with his hands and ankles tied. The groom who had been set to watch him had fallen asleep in the master's high-backed chair. Stephen cut Tad loose and led him to the front door.

"You can go now," Stephen told him.

"What's happened?" the boy asked suspiciously as he stepped into the street.

"There's been a fire at your house. The shed burned. Your father will be wanting you." Stephen tossed him his knife. "You can get out Linney gate. Just be sure to shut it behind you."

"Asshole," the boy spat and ran off toward the gate.

Stephen returned to the hall, climbed the stairs and went down the hallway to Olivia's bedroom. A manservant was posted outside the door, who said, "Sir, Lady Margaret left strict orders — no one's to go in."

"That doesn't apply to me," Stephen said and brushed by him to enter the room.

Olivia lay on a big canopied bed with the covers drawn up to her chin. Margaret was seated beside her, applying a linen compress to her bruised face, which was illuminated by a single candle flickering on the night stand by the bed. Margaret whirled and stood up at his entrance.

"Stephen," she said with alarm. "Olivia's gravely hurt. She mustn't be disturbed."

"She needs to tell what she told Clement," Stephen said grimly. "I need to know. Now."

"I can't allow it. I'm sorry." Margaret balled her fists. "You must wait — at least till morning. Let her have her rest, I beg you."

There was a commotion at the door. It swung open. Walter appeared momentarily then stepped back and a thin, pinch-faced man in a black cloak entered, followed closely by a very short and very broad woman also in a black cloak but carrying a wooden box by a leather strap, an herbalist by the look of her.

"Ah, the physician," exclaimed Margaret. "Stephen, he's going to examine her now." She put a hand on his arm and pulled his head down to reach his ear. The lilac scent of her perfume made him giddy, despite his fatigue. She whispered, "She may have been violated."

It was a pointed demand for privacy. In the face of these requests, Stephen didn't feel he could object. He would have to wait until morning. He retreated to the hall, kicked the sleeping groom awake and confiscated the chair. Brooding, he tossed another split of oak on the fire. If Olivia had told Clement anything useful, morning might be too late to learn what it was and to profit from it himself. But there was nothing he could do about that.

Sometime later, he awoke to the gentle brush of a soft hand on his face and the scent of lilac. Margaret was leaning over him. Her hair had been taken down and fell over her shoulders in a heart-stopping tumble. The hall seemed to be empty, except for the two of them.

"Come to bed, Stephen," she smiled. "I know you're tired."

Taking his hand, she led him upstairs to her room.

They made love again that morning after they woke up and bathed each other in the basin. Margaret had never had a man bathe her before. The water brought by one of the servants was only warm rather than hot and the wash cloth raised goose pimples on her perfect skin. She grasped his shoulders, shuddering as he cleaned her stomach, buttocks, between her legs, and her thighs. She returned the favor eagerly, then drew him into bed once more. They did not leave the room till after the normal time for breakfast.

On the way down to the hall, Margaret paused at Olivia's room and went in. She did not let him follow. Stephen caught a glimpse of the short broad woman seated in a chair by the bed, and Olivia's pale, mottled face in the midst of the brown blossom of her hair, which was sprayed across the pillows. It was so neatly arranged that he was sure someone had combed it during the night. Then Margaret shut the door. She came out a quarter hour later to report that Olivia was sleeping and should not yet be disturbed.

Whatever they might do in private, their public behavior had to be circumspect and proper, no matter that the servants all knew what was going on. So at table, they acted as though there was nothing particular between them.

After breakfast, Stephen took his leave with normal cool courtesy, and the only thing that gave the game way was the fact Margaret followed him to the front door. When no one was looking, she grasped him around the waist and they kissed as fiercely as they had during the night.

"Send word as soon as Olivia wakes up, promise?" Stephen asked her in the doorway.

"I will," Margaret said. "Will you come back for dinner?"

"I can't promise that."

She looked disappointed. "Supper, then?"

"Supper," he promised, smiling.

He stepped out into the street.

She shut the door.

Stephen hesitated. He wasn't sure what to do now. He was certain that Olivia knew who had killed William Muryet. Whoever had done so was the person who had intended to buy the list from them. But that intention obviously had been false. The buyer decided to save his money by killing Muryet, taking the list, and then disappearing. Someone would only decide on such a ruthless course if he felt he had a safe place to run. Only a man from Montfort's party could feel so secure, and Stephen only knew one person cruel enough for such a course attached to Montfort: Nigel FitzSimmons.

But he had to be sure.

He had jumped to conclusions before and had been wrong.

He didn't want to be wrong about this.

But unless and until Olivia was ready to speak, there was nothing to go on.

He was too restless to return to the Broken Shield to wait for her to wake up. So he turned north and went through Linney Gate, which stood open now it was daytime.

The path wound down the hill between grassy fields, which were still green despite the fact that autumn was well along. It was late in the morning, the sun was high, the sky was clear, and it was unusually warm, almost springlike — a joyous day. Too joyous to be about the somber business of murder.

He limped down the path, with his bad foot aching already. He passed a woman struggling upward under the burden of a huge bag of cabbages, which she must be intending to sell. The path threaded between two yards, bounded on each side by wattle fences, of houses that fronted on Corve Street. A pair of women were washing laundry in a big tub in one of the yards. It had always struck Stephen as funny how wet clothes would trap bubbles of air when you pushed them into the water, and this laundry was no exception. The laundresses often played at smothering the bubbles by smacking or punching them while they sang. It was so warm that one of these laundresses climbed in the tub. They saw him watching. The girl in the tub, a pretty thing who enjoyed the attention, smiled and playfully raised her skirt so he could admire the lush columns of her thighs. Stephen saluted her and leaned against the fence to watch for a few moments. It reminded him of girls trampling wine grapes, a regular sight in Spain. He was glad to see people going about their business and being happy, untouched by the grim events of the last few days.

He reached Corve Street and turned north. There were several carts in the street, one bulging with hay that stood so high he was sure it wouldn't fit through the town gate where it was headed, another carrying barrels, a third hauling sheep tethered to the sides and looking none too happy about the ride. Stephen heard a horse trotting fast behind him, turned to look, and had to dodge out of the way as a post rider from the castle surged by, leather message tubes like those he had seen in Baynard's study bouncing from straps on his belt.

Before long, the Webbere house came into view around the bend in Corve Street. Stephen paused at the mouth of the alley and regarded the spot where Muryet had died.

Then he knocked on the front door.

A boy answered the door. Stephen recognized him as Webbere's young son. He called out to someone behind him, "Ma! That coroner man's back!"

"Mind your manners and ask him in," Mistress Webbere's voice called from within the house.

The boy held the door open and Stephen stepped into the large room that passed for the hall in such a modest house. And modest it was, although it was better appointed than the houses of many people of this class. Although the floor was hard-packed dirt, it was covered with fresh straw. There were four chairs arranged around a large oak table, two sideboards for storing linens and dinnerware, and a large fireplace where a low fire was burning and putting out quite a bit of heat. Mistress Webbere was seated on one of two benches before the fireplace mending one of the boy's socks.

"Go and play, Ivo," she said to the boy. Apparently she had him doing some chore or other because his face brightened at this unexpected release. He wasted no time in dashing out the front door.

"Bit warm for such a fire," Stephen said conversationally. He sank onto the bench opposite Mistress Webbere.

"Once autumn's here, I can't seem to get warm," Mistress Webbere said. "But you didn't come to talk about the weather."

"No. I think it's time you told me who really has been renting your room upstairs."

"I don't know what you mean."

"Don't pretend ignorance with me. I know you haven't been renting it to a countrywoman."

"You're misinformed, I'm afraid."

"You've been renting it to Olivia Baynard."

The only sign that he may have scored a hit was a slight downturn of Webbere's mouth at the corners. But she offered no explanation or answer.

Stephen said: "Howard Makepeese is dead — you must have heard the news. And Olivia Baynard may well follow soon if I do not find out the truth."

Several heartbeats passed. Then Webbere said, "I am sworn not to tell."

"If necessary and possible, I will keep your secrets."

She sighed. "But you cannot promise."

"No, I can't. A murder must be accounted for and something valuable that has been lost must be found. Your secrets may have to be sacrificed."

"They aren't my secrets. I was just pledged to keep them."

"And paid to do so, I imagine."

The corners of her mouth drooped again, but this time her eyes narrowed. Stephen felt a swell of triumph. He had scored a hit. She said, "It's a sad story, a woman's story. You probably won't understand or sympathize, being just a man."

"I will try not to condemn or judge," Stephen said.

"All right, then. As you probably know, Mistress Baynard married her husband because she was desperate. You cannot imagine the fear she felt — her brother hanged and quartered as an embezzler of royal funds entrusted to him, his lands and hers confiscated and sold at auction. She had nowhere to go and no man of the gentry would have her. She faced destitution on top of humiliation. Then Baynard rescued her — a man on the brink of old age who lacked an heir and she a fertile young woman not yet twenty. He didn't care about her past, only about what she might bring to his future.

"But he let her know from the beginning that she was meant to be nothing more than a brood mare, a wife in name and law, but not in reality. Can you conceive of how bitter such a thing is? To be regarded as only property, as the vessel for another man's lust, not of his affection or respect?

"She quickly grew to understand her mistake, but there wasn't anything she could do. Frankly, I doubt she would have left Baynard even if she could have done. Some women will put up with the worst humiliation for position and wealth, and wealth she had if not the position she craved."

"But she still wanted affection," Stephen said.

"Yes. Is that so strange? To want love?"

"No. But to turn to Makepeese . . ."

"Ah, yes. Another mistake. He was a smooth one, and not lacking in looks and charm. She made the mistake of lying with him early in the marriage."

"But they kept it secret. Olivia hired your room, and crept out in the night through Linney Gate for her rendezvous."

Webbere affirmed his guess with a nod and a slight smile. "It only lasted two weeks before she saw through him. But it was too late after their first night together. She had to pay for his silence after she broke it off — which he took rather well, by the way. It did not cost her a lot, however. Howard was content with my room."

"So he used it to meet other women?"

"He had gained a taste for gentry women now that he had caught one, even for a short time. My room was a place he could carry on in secret."

"And her husband found out."

"No, I don't think he ever did. She was quite circumspect. She only came after dark. Even her own servants were unaware, Howard said. He was quite proud of that. He feared revelation as much as she, you know. Had Baynard found out, he'd have turned Clement on him." She shuddered. "A vicious man, Clement. He enjoys causing pain."

"What did Howard tell you about the list?"

Webbere shook her head sadly. "He never spoke about it. You can find many things to criticize about him, but he did keep secrets."

"Was Howard here the night Muryet died?"

"I believe he was, yes."

"In the room."

"I would imagine so. I heard someone moving about up there. I assume it was him."

Stephen stood up. "I'd like to see the room."

"Very well."

Webbere led him outside and round to the alley, where they mounted the stairs, moving with an odd slowness, as if they were in a funeral procession. The loose board on the stair had been replaced, and Stephen was a bit surprised to see that the latch on the door was new as well. The iron was fresh and black without a spot of rust, and the catch on the inside, although old, had been nailed to a fresh, yellow block of wood that had been inserted specially for it in an otherwise old and gray door frame. Oddly, the latch had provision for locking with an iron pin, which hung from a chain above the latch itself. The pin itself was twisted, obviously damaged when someone had forced the door, breaking the latch.

The room itself was spare, but with features that suggested an attempt to alleviate some of its poverty. There was a circular wool rug of red and blue on the floor, something one hardly ever saw in houses, a rocking chair, and a feather mattress on the bed with real feather pillows as well. He was willing to bet that Webbere didn't sleep on so fine a mattress. The fireplace across the room was cold and the ashes had been swept out, leaving only a blackened spot to show that it had been used at all. There was a window by the fireplace. Stephen crossed over and threw open the shutters so there was some light to see. The window overlooked part of the roof of the house. He was about to turn away when something caught his eye. There was a long brown hair snagged on a splinter of the window frame. He ran his hands along the hair: it was as long as his arm, too long to have come from a man. He wound the hair into a band around his finger and put the band in his purse.

While Webbere stood by the door, watching with folded hands, Stephen went over the room with the same care he had used on Muryet's chamber at Baynard House: tapping panels in the walls, dismantling the bed, probing the mattress and the pillows. He even fingered the bricks of the fireplace for loose ones in case here was a secret compartment behind one of them, but they were solid in their mortar. Last, he climbed onto the rafters, which were wide substantial beams, and checked along them and in every cranny.

But it was all for nothing.

If Olivia or Howard had hidden the list here, he could not find it.

"Is Olivia still paying rent on this place?" he asked Webbere.

"She is paid up for the rest of this month," Webbere said primly, clearly a businesswoman who honored her commitments to the end.

Stephen went outside and began to descend the stairs.

A stocky figure turned into the alley from the street, followed by six muscular friends. They were all wearing swords.

It was Clement.

He grinned wolfishly.

He said, "Find anything? I rather thought not. Oh, and you're under arrest, by the way."

Chapter 23

"And what have I done to merit arrest?" Stephen asked coldly. He did not come down any farther but stayed where he was on the stairs. He thought quickly about his options. Webbere was a momentary obstacle behind him. He could be around her in no time. The door was latched but the pin securing the latch was not in place. The door would not slow him appreciably. And he had left the window open. He could be through it and onto the roof below it as fast as an eel evades the net — as fast as, he thought, Howard and Olivia had fled the night Muryet had died.

Clement seemed to read his mind. He spoke quickly to the men behind him. Two ran out of the alley. Clement said, "Miles and Herbert will be waiting for you if you're thinking about slipping out the window."

Clement had him checked. Stephen was confident that he could handle two men, but not if they were armed with swords when he was not. Any attempt to escape through the window and over the house and those two would cut him to ribbons. He decided to brazen things out as far as he could. "I said, what have I done to merit an arrest?"

"Oh, you know very well. A small matter of arson and assault."

Stephen was stunned at the accusation. He had been certain that Will Thumper would be too concerned about inquiries into the contents of his storeroom to level such a charge. But then he realized that in all likelihood the storeroom was empty now, a barren testament to Thumper's poverty. Still, he said, "Who brings this charge?"

"Oh, come now, Stephen, don't be coy. It doesn't become you."

"You have no business condescending to me!"

Clement bowed, his mocking grin widening. "When his honor is done with you, you'll have no position, and I can condescend to you all I like — before you hang."

A crowd had begun to gather around the head of the alley as people drew together to see what was going on. Clement was not disturbed by the presence of the crowd. He'd do his awful work out of their sight. But he was inspired to show off.

Clement put his hands on his hips and swaggered at the foot of the stairs. He pointed his finger at Stephen. "Come on down, you blackguard. You can't escape the king's justice."

"The king's or yours, Clement? I'll trust myself to the king's justice but yours I have doubts about."

"Don't make me come get you!" Clement thundered. "You'll rue that decision!"

"Oh, I don't think you're the sort of man who likes to take on someone he can't bully. Come as you like."

Across the street Margaret, Walter, and James appeared on horses. They slid off and began to push through the crowd.

If they had come to help, they were not in time. Clement was not inclined to trade words after all. He drew his sword and mounted the stairs. Mistress Webbere gasped and clambered up to the top in a flurry of skirts and naked ankles.

Stephen did not follow her. He drew his dagger and waited to see what Clement would do.

"Going to defend yourself with that little needle, are you," Clement said with relish.

Stephen held his arms wide in answer.

Clement lunged with the sword, driving the point upward toward Stephen's stomach.

Stephen pivoted to his left with the calm assurance of one on the dance floor, avoiding the deadly point as though it was no more dangerous than a finger, and helping the flashing blade aside with his dagger.

Clement's momentum carried him forward and he stumbled on the stairs at Stephen's feet.

Stephen kicked him hard in the face. Pain lanced through his bad foot at the impact.

Clement toppled over backward and tumbled to the bottom of the stairs. He lay in almost exactly the same spot where Muryet's body had been found. The crowd, which had been silent, burst out with a cheer. Two of Clement's men helped him to his feet. Clement wiped blood from his mouth and panted, his face writhing with anger and humiliation.

Stephen leaned over and retrieved Clement's sword, which had fallen upon a step. Now that he had a sword, he was not as helpless as before. But his mind was not on fighting. It was far away. Something Clement had said was rattling in his mind like the shard of a pitcher that had been broken and needed to be fitted into its proper place so the pitcher could be mended. Then it clicked.

Stephen descended the steps. Clement's men drew their swords. The crowd rustled backward to give them room to fight. Stephen stopped on the last step just as Margaret burst through the cordon of spectators. He said, "You killed Muryet, Clement. Right there, where you're standing now. You knew he had Baynard's list. How did you find out? Did Lucy tell you?"

"He knew because when he was in jail he told Muryet to make sure it was still there," Margaret said. "But instead of keeping it safe for Clement, Muryet took the list to his mistress."

Stephen nodded. "Olivia is awake, then."

"And she has told everything," Margaret said with bitter triumph.

Stephen stepped off the stair, the sword's point toward the ground, but only a fool would think it out of position, for this was the fool's guard, deceptive and ready for any threat. He said, "Ah, I see. You told him what it was worth. You told him it was more than parchment and scribbles. It was a great fortune. You thought he would do as you asked. He always had. But he betrayed you — he betrayed you in your time of greatest need."

The tight line of Clement' mouth told Stephen he had struck the truth.

Stephen went on, "Perhaps you thought you might profit from the list rather than turning it over to your master's replacement. But your arrest for murder spoiled any such plan. Because then you needed it to bargain for your freedom by promising Valence the list. Only you found it gone. Oh, you were in trouble then."

"Lies! Slander!" Clement snapped with convincing indignation. "There is no truth here, only the desperate words of a man who seeks to avoid condemnation!"

"But how did you know about the window, Clement?" Stephen said ominous calm.

"Window?" Clement blustered. "Of what importance is a window?"

"It is the key to your guilt. You knew to have men cover it because it offered an escape route. You knew it offered the possibility of escape because Howard Makepeese had fled through it. You saw him there on the landing where Mistress Webbere is now watching as you killed Muryet. You saw him flee into the apartment, you broke the door down — and you found him gone, that window the only possible way out."

"A fairy story, not fit to entertain children," Clement snorted. He made a play of composure that might have convinced many of those watching, but did not convince Stephen.

"There was another witness, however," Stephen said. "One who still lives."

"Stephen!" Margaret warned sharply.

Clement was coolly defiant. "Bring forth this witness."

"Why, Clement, you already know her involvement. Olivia Baynard will give her testimony when it is time," Stephen said, despite the warning from Margaret. His job was to catch murderers, not to protect thieves.

Clement remained remarkably calm. Only the twitching of the corners of his eyes with every utterance betrayed his distress. "She knows nothing," he said.

"Oh, she knows much. She saw you, as well, no doubt through the cracked door. She left one of her hairs on the window frame as she, with Howard, fled from you over the roof. You knew she was involved after having us followed to

Marlbrook, where you discovered Howard hiding on land once held by her family. He would only have hidden there if she concealed him — which meant that she knew about the list. People are more likely to believe her than you think. She may have suffered misfortune, but she is a lady and has borne it with dignity. People respect that. They will listen to her. You know this. In fact, you sought to have her killed because you knew she would be believed."

The color drained from Clement's face. He took a faltering step back, then another. He hadn't anticipated that there might have been another witness. After Makepeese's death he must have felt much safer. But his confidence now crumbled before their eyes.

Stephen advanced toward the retreating Clement. His voice, like his steps, came implacably. "You killed Muryet because he wouldn't give you the list. He was more loyal to his mistress than to you, and you couldn't stand that. You had frightened him into obedience all your time at Baynard House, but when it mattered most, he could not be frightened. You wanted his death then more than you wanted the list. You would have killed Makepeese, too, if Lucy hadn't done your work for you. And you plotted with Will Thumper to cut Olivia's throat to silence her because she knew what you had done."

The crowd shrank from Clement as he backed away and his men stood dumbfounded, not knowing what to do. Then hands reached for Clement to take possession of his body in the time-honored way of the hue-and-cry, the public duty to apprehend criminals.

The realization that the crowd had decided against him broke any remaining resolve Clement might have harbored. He turned and ran, pushing aside those who stood between him and flight, to dash down Corve Street, his short coat flapping. Several men pursued him, but though he ran on legs fueled by fear, he could not outdistance them. As he came abreast of St. Leonard's chapel, which stood by the street a short distance away, he ducked through the door, knocking off his feet a deacon, who was sweeping the walkway. The pursuit stopped at the door, while three men went round to the rear to prevent Clement from escaping that way.

"Should we fetch him out?" one of the guards at the door called back to Stephen, who waved and shook his head. Clement might not be entitled to mercy under the law, but he was entitled to sanctuary fairly claimed.

Clement's flight and claim of sanctuary were as good as any confession as far as the neighborhood was concerned. People came up and congratulated Stephen and slapped him on the back. Stephen muttered his thanks, to be polite if nothing else. He didn't feel as though he merited congratulations. He'd stirred up many lives and probably ruined Olivia's. That merited regret, not celebration.

Gradually the crowd broke up as people drifted back to work and the children to play. Clement's helpers were the first to go, hurrying down Corve Street toward the gate to town, no doubt to carry the news of Clement's fall to Valence. Before long, only Stephen, Margaret, James and Walter remained at the head of the alley.

"So, after all this, it's still missing then?" Margaret asked, dismayed. "Muryet carried the secret of its whereabouts to his grave?"

"It is missing." Stephen added, "But I think I know where it is." He had spoken softly, hardly aware of saying the words, for random, seemingly unconnected thoughts had begun to swirl in his mind: an evening's rain, a damp wool coat, a wooden peg with a missing waxy cylinder for carrying documents, a lost dagger, floating laundry – and a fish in a barrel.

Margaret's mouth opened in astonishment as if she had a question on her lips, although none came out, as Stephen turned to the big wooden barrel filled to the brim with drainage water from the eaves. The water appeared black as obsidian and nothing was visible in the barrel except green wisps of algae growing against the sides. The fish he thought he had seen there was gone, or seemingly so. And for a moment, his heart lurched at the prospect that he might be wrong. Stephen pulled up his sleeve and plunged his arm into the blackness. The water was bitterly cold. He felt around. His fingers met nothing at first. Then he bumped something. There was a bit more fumbling until he caught it.

He drew out a long slender leather tube, the same sort of tube hanging from the shelves in Baynard's study, the kind of tube used to carry dispatches. Entangled in its strap and weighing it down was a dagger.

Stephen untangled the dagger. "This belonged to Muryet, I'm sure."

"And that —" Margaret began wide-eyed.

"A moment and we'll know for certain." Stephen fumbled with the bronze catch and opened the top of the tube. He inserted two fingers and drew out rolls of parchment. Except for one edge, they were remarkably dry, the writing on them legible.

"It is them," Margaret breathed.

"Yes, I'm glad to say it is."

"But why are they not ruined?"

"Tubes like these are waxed on the outside to keep documents from getting wet. The seal traps the air within especially when it's immersed upside down — rather like air bubbles are trapped in clothes in a laundry tub."

"How did you know?"

"A guess. Just a guess. The fact Clement didn't have the lists — and neither did anyone else — meant Muryet must have hidden them before his death. I'll wager Muryet took the documents down from the room expecting to meet the buyer. He found Clement instead. He had enough time to weigh the satchel down and hide it in the barrel without Clement seeing him. Muryet probably thought to retrieve it as soon as Clement left. Unfortunately, things did not turn out as he'd planned."

"Things so often do not turn out as you'd planned," Margaret said heavily. Then she brightened. "May I see them?" She eased close, a pliant expression on her face. "May I see what you have so long striven for?"

Stephen stopped her with a hand on her shoulder, holding her at length. "No."

She was shocked at the unexpected refusal. Her eyes searched his face but found only coldness. For a moment, he thought he saw hurt in her eyes, but if it was there, it did not linger long. Her own cold comprehension took its place.

"I see. Well, I have my duty, too." She stepped back and spoke sharply, "James! Walter! Get them! Let's be done!"

But neither James nor Walter moved.

Margaret's mouth pressed together in fury at their insubordination.

Wincing at her fury, James said reluctantly, "My lady, you have no idea what he's capable of. I saw last night. It was magnificent. Four men could not take him. We two have no chance — and now he has a sword."

That sword was leaning up against the barrel. Stephen made no move to take it up, but it wasn't far from his hand if he needed it. He said, "You're the buyer, the one whom Muryet was to meet that night."

Margaret's small fists balled in anger and frustration. She nodded.

"Would Olivia have told me this too? Is that why you worked so hard last night and this morning to keep me from speaking to her?"

"She did not know at first. James and Walter dealt for me only with Muryet. But later she knew."

Stephen smiled sadly. "After you returned from Marlbrook."

"How do you know that?"

"Because you made the same connection Clement did when he realized Howard was hiding on Marlbrook land — a connection you did not share with me when you easily could have done. That hut, that was the place you used to meet secretly with Olivia when you were children, isn't it."

Margaret nodded slowly, almost involuntarily.

Stephen went on, "So you rushed back to Ludlow thinking to pry out of her the last of her secrets, perhaps believing she knew the lists' whereabouts, confessing a few of your own secrets to make it easier for her to part with hers. You couldn't allow her to speak with me then because I'd see you for the rival you are — a more dangerous rival, I think, than Clement."

"I do not want to be your rival, Stephen."

"As you say, things so often do not turn out as you'd planned." He looked up and down the street to see if anyone was watching. Even Mistress Webbere had disappeared. He stuffed the rolled up parchments back in the case. Then, leaving the cap off, he plunged the case into the frigid water of the barrel.

"What are you doing!" Margaret cried. She rushed to the barrel and tried to wrench the tube from his grasp. But she was not strong enough and succeeded only in getting the both of them drenched.

"Saving lives," Stephen said.

He removed the tube, which was still filled with water he did not pour out.

Margaret gaped at him, aghast.

Then Stephen hefted the sword, pleased with its lightness and balance. Carrying tube and sword, he strode around Margaret to the middle of the street and marched as quickly as his aching bad foot would allow toward Corve Gate.

He did not look back.

Even though he wanted to — badly, very badly.

Chapter 24

Stephen forced himself to walk at an ordinary pace until he rounded the bend in Corve Street that took him out of sight of the Webbere house. With a swift backward glance to see if they were coming or not, he quickened his pace as near to a run as he could comfortably get.

He turned in at the path that threaded between houses and up through yards and fields to Linney Gate. Ahead, to his surprise, he saw Gilbert Wistwode, who was hurrying down the path as fast as his waddle could carry him.

"My word, Stephen!" Gilbert gasped, his exertions of last night having done nothing to get him in shape for this. He grasped Stephen by the elbows and shook him in his delight to find him. "You're all right! You're free!" He glanced warily about. "I came to warn you. Come here where you'll be safe, at least for the moment. We'd heard you are to be arrested. They said you were seen heading to Corve Street. I deduced you were continuing your investigations at the Webbere house. What have you discovered? Oh —" he said, his eyes falling on the leather tube. "You found something. Is that it?"

Stephen nodded. "There's been a mishap."

"I can see that. It's sopping." Gilbert took the tube from Stephen. "You haven't even bothered pouring out the water."

"I thought it best if it soaked a while longer."

"But, but, but — you won't be able to read a thing. Why, water dissolves ink!"

"Clever of me, don't you think?"

"You've gone mad!"

"Wasn't it you who told me that the list will mean the deaths of men? I should have stolen it when I had the chance. Then Muryet at least would be alive, perhaps even Makepeese and poor Lucy. It's strange, isn't it, how the best intentions can cause more harm than good."

"You did what you thought best at the time. Think about your present and your future and — I say, why are you walking about with a sword?"

"Clement was kind enough to lend it to me. He doesn't have any use for it now."

"Clement?" Gilbert sputtered. "Stop speaking in riddles."

"That wasn't a riddle."

"Well, it was damned unclear enough to be one."

Stephen couldn't help laughing. He put his arm around Gilbert's shoulders as they climbed the rise to town.

They reached Linney Gate just as he finished the story. Stephen paused and poured the water out of the leather tube into the ditch. "That should do it, I hope. What does parchment look like after it's soaked for a week?"

"I have no idea. Probably wetter than that." Gilbert's hands twitched over the top of the tube. "May I?" he asked.

"Might as well." Stephen gave him the tube, although he itched to be moving.

Gilbert slid out the sheets halfway and unfurled a corner. "Only smudges left. Now how will you placate Valence? If he can't have his list, he'll have your head instead. There's already been quite a call for it this morning, I understand."

"Will Thumper's fire," Stephen said.

"Yes. You won't mention that I was there, will you? Thank goodness. Listen, young man, this is no business to take lightly. Arson and house-breaking are serious matters, and he appealed against you on both counts before Valence this morning. People hang for that, you know."

"Yes, Clement mentioned something like that."

"Well, you ought to know — you studied the law!"

"Damn the law. We haven't got time for it." Stephen hurried through the gate.

"No time for the law? What kind of nonsense is that? You're not thinking about turning outlaw are you? Good Lord! What a frightful brigand you'll make. I'm warning you, I'll not be a part of that! You may not be law abiding, but I am! I am, I really am."

In only a few strides, Stephen reached the front door to Baynard House. He didn't bother knocking. He just opened the door and went in. He was crossing the great hall before any of the servants took notice that the house had been invaded, and when they saw the look on his face and the sword in his hand, they all fled to the rear of the house.

Stephen mounted the stairs two at a time and went to Olivia's room.

He didn't bother knocking at this door, either.

Olivia was awake, propped against pillows, a cup in her lap. Her hair was combed and tied behind her head, the picture of matronly neatness. But her face was puffy and badly bruised and her lips were cut and swollen.

Stephen sat on the edge of the bed and laid the document case beside him.

"You found it," Olivia said.

"I found something," Stephen said.

"That's — that's not it? That's not the list?"

"It is the case and the documents you delivered to Muryet last Thursday night."

She was silent, her eyes locked on his.

Stephen went on, "But this case contains a copy. A copy you made."

"I confess, I gave Muryett the list that night to deliver to the buyer's agents. But it was not a copy."

"I've seen the original, Olivia, or have you forgotten? In this house, in the room down the hallway. This —" he patted the document case "— was in a different hand, not your husband's hand, and changes had been made."

"Ch-changes?"

"There are names crossed out on the original, the names of men who died or were murdered. When you copied it over, you didn't copy those names. I remember one of them very well. It was that of Patrick Carter. You recall him — the poor fellow your husband and Clement killed in Ludford last month."

Olivia's cheek twitched.

Stephen said gently, "It's true, isn't it."

Olivia nodded, a mere jerk of the head, but it was a confession nonetheless.

"Where is it now?" Stephen asked.

"I gave it to Margaret."

"You just gave it to her?"

"Last night. After she deduced that I had it. I had no idea she had been sent to recover it and she had no idea that I was the one selling it until the end. But she promised her help and her lord's protection instead of silver."

"Who would that be?"

"Nigel FitzSimmons. You are acquainted with him, I understand."

"I know him, but not well." It saddened Stephen to think that Margaret owed allegiance to such a ruthless man as Nigel FitzSimmons. She was harder at the core and more capable of deception than he had thought. She had known, then, that what he found in the rain barrel was a copy. But she had been just as keen to keep it out of Valence's hands as the original, for even the copy could do great damage to her faction. She must have wanted to shout for joy when he plunged the copy back in the barrel, yet she never gave a hint of it.

"One last thing," Stephen said.

"Oh?"

"What were you doing at Mistress Webbere's house that night? You meant to deal with the buyer through your agent, Muryet, like any lady would. There was no need for you to be present."

Olivia smiled wanly. "I kept the list hidden there. Under a loose floorboard where no one would ever think to look. Only I knew."

Stephen slid off the bed and strode out of Olivia's room, nearly colliding with Gilbert, who blocked the door, his mouth agape in astonishment. "Out of the way," Stephen said more harshly than he intended. "They'll be here any minute. We have to find it."

"Oh, dear Lord," Gilbert said.

"Keep her there!" Stephen ordered, meaning Olivia, as he ran to Margaret's room. "Don't let her give the alarm!"

The thick green glass on the windows of the guest room emitted an eerie glow, as if he had suddenly fallen under the sea. It was much as he had left it this morning, except the big canopy bed, its posts painted red and blue, had been made.

There was only one place the list could reasonably be. Stephen shut the door and crossed to Margaret's traveling trunk. It was a huge thing that took two men to lift. These trunks were big because people of her class practically lived out of them, and they often held everything they owned except weapons and dinnerware. He opened the lid, which Margaret had not bothered to lock, a circumstance that caused a pang of doubt. Would she really have left so valuable a thing in an unlocked trunk? Gowns were neatly folded on top. He ran his fingers over the lid to check for secret compartments, then along the inside walls. Nothing. He burrowed down through the mass of clothing, feeling for the cringle of parchment or the waxy coolness of a document case. Still nothing. He began to fret that he had made a serious mistake. She might have hidden it somewhere else in the house.

Then at one corner at the bottom, his fingers met a square leather case, not round as he had been expecting.

He hauled out the case. It was flat and closed with a flap and was unwaxed.

He opened the flap.

There was parchment inside. He drew it partway out — and saw he had found what he was looking for. Baynard's original list.

He breathed a sigh of relief.

The door opened.

He turned to see who it was.

Margaret stood there.

She stepped in and to the side.

Walter was behind her with a loaded crossbow. He pointed the weapon at Stephen's navel.

Behind them, Stephen could see that James had Gilbert's arm twisted behind his back.

"Oh, Stephen," Margaret said. "I knew you were too smart for your own good. It will be the death of you, if you aren't careful." She held out her hand. "I'll have that. It's mine now. Come, don't hesitate. You're checkmated. I've won. You're not one of those men who hates being bested by a woman, are you?"

When he still hesitated, she added, "I'll let you make another copy. You can pass that off to Valence."

Still he hesitated. Margaret was losing her patience. She balled her fists. "Stephen, I'll have to let Walter shoot. I don't want to do that. Please!"

There wasn't anything he could do, really. There was nowhere to run. A step forward or backward and Walter would drill him with a quarrel. The thought of what a quarrel could do at close range made Stephen's stomach curl. As a boy, he had shot a deer at close range. The quarrel had gone clear through its body and lodged in a tree behind it.

He held out the square leather case.

Margaret reached for it.

Gilbert chose that moment to stamp on James' foot. James yelped and involuntarily loosened his grip. Gilbert, whom no one would take for a fighting man, drove an elbow into James' stomach.

Walter glanced back to see what the commotion was about.

Stephen saw his opportunity. He threw Clement's sword at Walter as if it was a spear. Walter could have shot him down right then, but he chose survival before impalement and stepped out of the way. The sword sailed passed him, through the door, and stuck in the wall on the other side of the hallway, narrowly missing James as he fought with Gilbert.

While Walter dodged the sword, Stephen jumped through the window, shielding his head with the leather case.

He had never jumped through a glass window before and had no idea what to expect. He half thought it might be as hard as a stone wall, and although it wasn't, it still gave him a terrific thump. The panes were set in a lattice of lead, which held for an agonizing moment, and then showered him with fragments as it gave way.

As he fell, not knowing what lay on the ground below, he sensed rather than saw a crossbow quarrel hiss by his ear.

Pinwheeling his arms, he plunged off balance, not centered over his feet. But this proved to be fortunate, for it forced him to roll with the impact. He climbed to his feet, aching in a multitude of places, aware of warm wetness on his head and an ear, and deeply glad he had not landed on his head.

He collected the round tube and the square case and ran limping to the wall separating the Baynard's yard from College Lane. It was a high wall, so tall he could barely reach the top even with a leap. But he managed to secure a grip and pulled himself up.

He looked back to see Margaret leaning out of the remains of the window. "Give my regards to your friend Nigel," he called.

She drew back and Walter replaced her with his crossbow.

Stephen slipped over the wall before Walter could shoot again.

There were people in College Lane — a woman struggling through Linney Gate under a load of hay which she was carrying on her back; a priest entering the grounds of St. Laurence Church; a matron with a gaggle of maids and a groom streaming toward him. They all regarded him in shock as if he was a demon that had just sprung out of the ground. It was his appearance, of course: bloody and without a hat.

Stephen tried to ignore them and act as if nothing was the matter.

Then Gilbert emerged from the front door of Baynard House. He smoothed the collar of his coat in a self-satisfied, merchantly way, and joined Stephen in the street. This seemed to convince the onlookers that something other than criminal activity was afoot, for Gilbert was a respected merchant and not to be suspected of involvement in lawbreaking.

As Stephen limped up College Lane to High Street with Gilbert at his side, he heard the matron cluck, "Men, always fighting. It's disgraceful — in the middle of the day yet!"

Stephen nodded to her as she passed. "Good morning, mistress," he said cheerfully.

"Good morning," she said stiffly, embarrassed that he had spoken her and that she had to answer him in return.

"She's right, you know," Gilbert said. "You are a disgrace." He took out a handkerchief and tried to wipe off some of the blood. "Well, I don't think that did much good. You'll have to wait until we get home."

The middle of the day. Yes. It would be dinner time at the Broken Shield. He could literally smell the mutton pie. He said, "You owe me a kettle of Edith's best, remember?"

"Oh, so I do. So I do. Goodness. We better hurry then, if we're to get home while there's some left."

They crossed High Street and entered Broad Street. A spring of a sort returned to Stephen's step. He was going home and he was glad.

Chapter 25

Will Thumper withdrew his plea against Stephen Attebrook for arson and house-breaking. He claimed that Clement had threatened him with death unless he brought the suit. Nevertheless, despite the claim of duress, Thumper's confession exposed him to a counter-plea for false swearing, which was almost as bad as homicide. Attebrook could have had legal satisfaction, but let the matter die.

Clement agreed to abjure the realm rather than face the hangman, a decision he was lucky to be able to make, since it enabled him to escape the consequences of two homicides and the displeasure of one of the country's leading jurists. He was assigned the departure point of Bristol, and given four days to reach it. But he never appeared there, as far as anyone knew. The following spring a traveler leaving the Bristol road south of Hereford to urinate in the woods discovered a skeleton among the undergrowth. It still wore the gray woolen shift of an abjurer and a heavy silver signet ring found with the bones caused everyone to believe this was Clement.

Valence was, predictably, furious that Baynard's list was destroyed by immersion. Fearing a trick, he was not immediately inclined to take Attebrook's word that the sodden, smeared parchments presented to him were the genuine article. But he reluctantly accepted fate when told there was a witness to the list's discovery in Webbere's rain barrel — the Lady Margaret de Thottenham, who corroborated the story to one of Valence's agents that very same day.

As for that lady and Olivia Baynard, they were seen leaving Ludlow late on a Thursday afternoon shortly after the leave-taking of Valence's representative, departing the Galdeford Gate and disappearing east toward Worcester. Little was heard in town again about Olivia. Some months later a man posing as her agent negotiated the sale on her behalf of the house and the rights to the burghage plot on which it sat. And about the same time, it was rumored that she had married a gentryman from Northumbria. Two or three people in town hoped that the rumor was true and that she had finally found a measure of happiness in life.

Harry the beggar acquired a handsome squarish leather case, which he used for carrying his belongings. He refused to say where he got it. "Matter of privilege," he claimed when one questioner persisted in knowing the identity of his benefactor. Because of his situation, no one thought it reasonable to accuse him of theft.

The Friday morning after the ladies' departure, Stephen Attebrook received a package. It was long and slender and accompanied by a note. The note was written in an elegant practiced hand. More oddly yet, it was in Latin rather than French or English. It said simply, "To Stephen, your obedient servant Passer, greetings. — I believe this is yours by right of battle. It would be wrong for us to take it, so I return it to you with my compliments." Stephen let the note rest on his lap. Passer was Latin for sparrow. He knew only one person who could be called that.

When Attebrook opened the package, he found Clement's sword.

Made in the USA
Lexington, KY
19 May 2012